A NOVEL

THROUGH THE TURN

SCOTT DUNN

GRAYHOUSE PUBLISHING

Grayhouse Publishing

Copyright 2004 by Scott Dunn
Cover design by Chuck Snider

ISBN 0-9710076-2-4

Manufactured in the United States of America

— To Leta and Thomas

It's better now.

COMPANY DIRECTIVE
March 7

Kevin Mitchell climbed into my Ford Explorer. His blond hair was still dark with moisture. As always, he wore a jacket with our company logo on it. This morning it was the green fleece.   I had jackets with our company logo too. But I didn't wear them anymore. It felt like a lie.

"Ready for another team meeting?" Kevin asked.

"I hate team meetings," I said, backing out of his driveway.

"You just hate getting up early."

He was right. Seven o'clock on a dark March morning was no kind of fun. But it wasn't the time. It was the waste of time. If I'm stuck working, I want to be productive. Team meetings rarely were.

Kevin and I were sales reps for Nucroix, a large supplier of spray equipment for the agricultural and turf markets. He thought we had the best jobs in the world. The company actually paid us to drive around in SUVs, which they provided, and talk to people.

"If Nucroix wants to pay me to eat lunch today, I'll let them," he said. "Now pull over."

I stopped at a Shell station so Kevin could buy a can of Skoal, which he'd promised his wife he'd quit, and a 16-ounce Diet Coke. Kevin's morning ritual was to drink his pop quickly, then have a chew.

Addictions satiated, Kevin got down to business. "So tell me, did it happen?"

I knew what he meant. We'd only discussed it 20 times the past three weeks. "Not this again."

Aggravated exhale. "Listen. I know it's none of my business. But I've been married for over ten years now. I would never even consider cheating on my wife. So I have to live vicariously through you." At 34, Kevin was five years my senior. "Have you at least seen her naked?"

My crooked grin gave away the answer.

"God, I wish I could tell people." I shot him a look. "I won't," Kevin said. "But I'd love to see their faces."

For the past month, I'd secretly been dating Lauren Reynolds, a 28-year-old promotions specialist from our Indianapolis office. She and I had been friends, but I never dreamed she'd date me. She tended to attract good-looking, rich guys. She actually attracted a wide range of men, but good-looking, rich guys were the ones who got in. But five weeks prior, she'd been offered a position with a competitor and wanted my opinion.

Jokingly, I'd said, "If you do leave Nucroix, there's no reason we can't go out."

"There's no reason even if I stay," she replied.

"What kind of panties does she wear?" Kevin asked.

"Now, come on."

"Listen, I dated Kylie five years before we got married. So it's been fifteen years since I've seen anyone's panties besides hers. I don't think I'm asking too much here."

Lauren's life revolved around impressing others, so she couldn't have normal underwear. They were designer panties purchased at a specialty boutique. They cost nearly $50 a pair. If Kevin knew this, we'd be discussing them all morning.

"Just plain white cotton."

"That surprises me. I figured she'd be more exotic." He thought for a moment. "She doesn't even have one thong for special occasions?"

"Don't you have any other single friends to live vicariously through?"

"No, actually, I don't. Besides, I think every guy in the company has wondered at one time or another what she'd be like. And now I can find out, first-hand, without doing anything to get in trouble."

"I'll tell you how it is. I feel trapped. She's already thinking marriage and shit. When we're together it's all about her trying to make me happy, which I know should be great. But it makes me uncomfortable. I want out."

"Let me get this straight." Kevin spat into the plastic bottle. "Lauren Reynolds wants nothing more than to please you, and you want out? Do I understand you correctly?"

"Yes."

"Then you're a homo. She's not just good-looking. She's smart. She's pleasant to be around. You should want to marry her."

The thought didn't sit right. For one thing, Lauren was a company woman. Eighty percent of our conversations were about Nucroix. She was obsessed with company hierarchy and politics. She loved having a career while I fantasized about losing my leg in a work-related accident.

"Here's the thing. If I did marry her, then this is the rest of my life. This is what I am."

"I got news for you, Vic. It's what you are anyhow."

"Maybe it is. Maybe it isn't."

We arrived at the Holiday Inn 10 minutes early. The only person who beat us was Marta, Miss "I want a promotion." She represented everything I hate about corporate politics. She would compliment upper management on policies that were clearly absurd and then squeal on our team when we veered from that course. We only let her get away with it for one reason; she'd likely be our boss soon.

"I'm surprised to see you on time," Marta said, picking something off her green corduroy pants. "I figured everybody would be late today because Ted isn't going to be here."

Ted was our district manager.

Reggie came barging in eating an Egg McMuffin. "I'm not late." Reggie had no background, experience, or even interest in the turf industry. He was however, a very intelligent, well-spoken black man: something our company lacked. So the more Reggie stated he wasn't interested, the more his salary offer was upped. Reggie was my age and made $15,000 a year more than I did.

At 8:05, Tim sauntered in without excuses or an apology. He was 48 years old, and had been with the company more than 20 years. He didn't like his job; he hadn't for as long as I'd known him. He went through the motions, and each year his sales numbers got a little worse. Tim's youngest daughter was a junior in high school. He planned to work until she graduated from college.

Finally, at 8:20, Nub Tucker bolted into the room, trapping a stack of papers and a day timer against his large belly with one hand and holding his cell phone to his ear with the other.

"I know," Nub said into the phone. "Do you really want to do business with that slippery son-of-a-bitch?...I see...How much?...Is that a lot of money?...I'm just asking the question...All right, I'm at a meeting right now, but I'll be there first thing tomorrow...I'll take care of you...Yes, I mean financially... Okay...See you tomorrow."

Nub flopped into a chair. "I may have just saved a million-dollar account for the team." His red, wavy hair was always disheveled, presumably from overwork. Nub took pride in working longer days than anyone in the company. He could have cut those extended hours considerably with even the tiniest effort to get organized. That really didn't interest Nub. Working hard was how he defined himself. Let the Mama's boys work smart.

The meeting agenda only had one item, segmentation, and more importantly, how we could coerce our retailers into attending a three-day training meeting. Marta tapped a flip chart with her Sharpie.

"Let's start brainstorming ideas."

Reggie spoke up first. "My customers are really resisting this."

Tim quickly agreed. "Mine, too. They're busy with their own businesses."

"My customers would rather watch two monkeys fuck than come to this meeting," Nub said, his mouth full of doughnut.

Marta glared at him. "Well, we have to do something to get them there."

"Maybe we could rent two monkeys," I said.

"Let's keep this professional," Marta scolded. "Segmentation is company directive."

"Is there any way we could make it just a one-day meeting?" Kevin asked, hoping to ease everyone's pain.

"Absolutely not," Marta replied, shaking her Sharpie-filled fist. "People from headquarters have already scheduled three days."

For the next three hours our discussion never stayed on track. We debated anything and everything whether it related to segmentation or not. And even this lost cause couldn't go more than 20 minutes without being interrupted by Nub's cell phone, into which he talked loudly for several minutes each time.

At 11:15, as Nub completed his fifth call of the morning, Marta exploded. "Will you turn that thing off? We aren't accomplishing anything here."

"I have a competitor out there calling on our customers, trying to take our business," Nub said, biting hard on "our."

"You need to shut off your phone. Ted is going to call before lunch to see how we're doing on this," Marta said, biting equally hard on "Ted."

That changed things. For about 30 minutes we got fairly serious about coaxing our clients into a bogus meeting. We had eight different bribes listed before Ted called.

Nub answered the hotel phone. "Hey boss...we're doing great...of course, everyone's on board...we're going to have a great meeting." Nub lied for a few more seconds before handing the phone to Marta so she could lie. After Ted hung up, we agreed by a vote of four to one to adjourn.

"We need to have another team meeting next week," Marta said.

"What for?" Tim asked.

Marta looked at him like he was an idiot. "What for? To handle the logistics of our training meeting."

"Hell," Nub said. "You can do that, Marta. You live for this shit."

Marta thought a moment. "Nah, we still have to meet."

Everyone groaned.

"It's not my fault," she said. "It's company directive."

"You tell your bosses at Nucroix to shove it up their asses!"

My first attempt at company directive was off and running. Marvin Fry's account was the biggest in my territory, and he bullied me with it. In the past three years, I had taken him and his family to Las Vegas, Myrtle Beach, and every major sporting event in the tri-state area. And he'd still sell me out for a nickel.

"Does Nucroix think they know more about my business than I do?" Marvin asked.

"No, of course not. They-"

"You're God damn right they don't!" Marvin lit a cigar. He smoked a cheap, vile brand. "I started this business and kept her afloat for 35 years. I've seen them all come and go. Name another independent who's been around as long as I have."

"There isn't one."

"You're God damn right there isn't!"

Marvin's office was filling with stink. "May I open the door?"

"No. My wife can't stand the smoke." His wife was also the secretary and the bookkeeper and the cleaning lady and ... "Do you think I don't know my customers?"

"No, I think you do."

"You're God damn right I do! You don't stay in business as long as I have by not. Now you're going to come in here and tell me I've been doing it wrong all these years."

"No, of course not Marvin."

"You said three-day *training* meeting on, uh, sectioning off."

"Segmentation," I corrected.

"College word," Marvin scoffed. He glanced at his watch. "Explain it to me one more time." Marvin leaned back in his leather chair and put both hands behind his fat, pink head. I hated kissing this conceited pig's ass.

"Well, Marvin, Nucroix wants to segment your end-users into different categories, then offer each category a unique product bundle that fits their needs. Some guys want the newest stuff and are willing to pay for it. Some guys want a lot of service. Some guys only care about price. The meeting is about how to identify each category and what to offer them."

Marvin rocked forward, spewing smoke in my direction. "Vic, how old are you?"

"Twenty-nine."

"No offense, but you don't know shit. I've been doing this kind of thing for more years than you've been alive. Literally. All you have to do is create a couple options and price them right. Your customer will purchase what he wants. You don't have to give him a name. It's real easy."

I hate to admit it, but Marvin was 100 percent right.

"But your company's too arrogant to listen." Again, right on the money. "I know it's not your fault, Vic, but if you want to do business with people, you have to show them respect. A customer can buy from anybody. You know what makes him loyal? Integrity. That's why we've lasted and the other guy hasn't. Integrity." His watch alarm beeped. It was noon. "You buying lunch?"

"Sure," I said. "Where would you like to go?"

"How's about the titty bar?"

Ah, yes. Integrity.

After an afternoon of unbearable company, way past their prime dancers, and a surprisingly good tenderloin, I called it quits for the day and went home. The thoughts of spewing Nucroix rhetoric at another customer numbed me. Seven years with the same company isn't a lifetime, but it is long enough to know whether or not you enjoy your work, and I didn't. But I couldn't think of a better job. At least not one I was qualified for.

The telephone rang, but I didn't answer it. You never answer your phone on a weekday before six. What if it's a customer? God forbid people think you're not working. The machine picked up, relayed my message, and beeped.

"Hey, Vic, this is Doug." Doug was the manager of my fourth largest account, and a really good guy. "I know this isn't your fault, but Nurcroix screwed up my invoice again. So I called your billing department and told them I wasn't paying until they got it right. Now today I got a letter in the mail saying they've put a credit freeze on my account. This is ridiculous. I'm canceling all my Nucroix business. Sorry, I know this isn't your fault."

I needed to call Doug back and straighten this mess out, and I would eventually. At the moment however I seemed to be frozen. I stared out my window at a goose pecking around for what had to be 10 minutes. It made me curious. What did that goose think of his life, out in the cold, scraping for food? At first it seemed unenviable. But the more I thought about it, the more I didn't think that bird had it so bad. It had never heard of team meetings or marketing plans or company directives. It just knew it was hungry.

I remembered reading something similar in the Bible, and decided to look it up. It took me several minutes to actually find my Bible and twice as long after that to locate this passage. Matthew 6:26-27, *Look at the birds: they do not plant seeds, gather a harvest and put it in barns; yet your Father in heaven takes care of them! Aren't you worth much more than birds? Can any of you live a bit longer by worrying about it?*

I had easily read that passage 50 times in my life, and it never really carried any significance for me. But now I got it. I didn't have to work for Nucroix. I'd saved up my money. Outside of my mortgage, I had no debt. There was nothing stopping me from quitting. That had never occurred to me until right then. But it was like a ton of bricks off my shoulders. Not only could I quit, I was going to. Immediately.

I had five days of vacation left. I would take it, then give my notice the day I returned. I sent a work email to all those concerned. Next week, I'm off limits.

I received a response from Marta.

```
Subj: Bad timing
Date: March 8
From: mboyd@nucroix.com
To: vwalker@nucroix.com
     Just for the record, I want you to
know that I think now is an unfortunate time
to take an "impulse" vacation.  We have a
very important meeting next month.
```

I clicked on reply: Tough shit! That felt fantastic.
Marta's response came very quickly.

```
Subj: Bad timing
Date: March 8
From: mboyd@nucroix.com
To: vwalker@nucroix.com
     Don't get nasty with me. It's company
directive.
```

Two weeks later, Kevin and I headed back to the Holiday Inn for another team meeting. "How could you dump Lauren before lake season?" Kevin angrily poured the rest of his Diet Coke out the window. This was upsetting news. He needed a chew.

"I have to stay in a relationship just because you want to see Lauren in a bikini?"

"Yes!" he yelled. "I've been looking forward to this all winter." Kevin had it all worked out in his head. He spent a lot of time at my lake house during the summers. Lauren naturally would, too. "What did you tell her?"

"My life is going in a new direction now, and it would probably make her crazy."

Kevin looked disgusted. He thought my reasoning was lame. "What new direction?"

"I'm quitting." Just saying it made me happy.

"Your job? When?"

"Today."

He spat in the Diet Coke container. A thin trail of brown saliva briefly linked his lip and bottle. "What are you going to do?"

"Water ski."

"No, I mean for work."

"I'm not going to work. I'm going to ski."

I'd lived on the lake for two years and had been too busy to appreciate it. I'd had moments, but I wanted a whole summer to just kick back and enjoy myself.

"First you tell me that I won't be seeing Lauren in a bikini. Now I have to know that every day while I'm working, you'll be playing on the lake. I'm beginning to hate you."

I laughed. I hadn't been this happy since college, if even then.

Kevin played with the power windows for a moment. Up. Down. Up. Down. Finally, up. "Are you sure you want to tell them right away? You should maybe give it some time."

At a red light I turned and faced him. "Let me ask you this. If you were going to die six months from now, would you want to know?"

Kevin's face turned pale. "You've got AIDS."

"I don't have AIDS."

"Are you sure?"

"I've never been tested, but... Wait. I'm not even going down that road with you. It's just a hypothetical question. Would you want to know?"

"I'm not sure," Kevin said, after spitting again. "I never think about stuff like that. Probably not."

I did think about stuff like that. I thought about it all the time. If I hated what I was doing, then I would want to know so I could change my life. But if I liked what I was doing, I wouldn't, because, well, why stop enjoying myself? And right now, I would want to know. That's why I wanted to announce it. So I couldn't get scared and back out.

"If you were dying of AIDS, you'd tell me, right?"

"I'm fine," I assured him. "But why do you keep saying AIDS? Why not cancer or something like that?"

"I'm still trying to figure out why you dumped Lauren before lake season."

"And you know what else? I may not even get a job this fall. I've decided that I am not going to work again until I find my true calling."

"You're true calling?" Kevin said, quite unmoved. "Just how do you intend to find this 'true calling' of yours?"

I'd actually thought this through. "If you had a destiny, how do you think God would communicate it to you?"

"I don't know. In a dream or something," Kevin said.

"Not a dream. Our dreams," I really felt that I had it all figured out. "God communicates our destiny by making us want something. We either then choose to fulfill this destiny or we talk ourselves out of it. 'That's not practical,' or 'I could never do that.' Then we settle for less, and that's what makes us so miserable."

Kevin bobbed his head. "I see. And I suppose God has spoken to you."

"Not that I know of. But for the first time in my life I am going to be open to it. I am doing everything I have a desire to do. That's how I'll find my life's work."

Kevin's cell phone rang. He looked at the caller ID and shut off the ringer. "Are you going to let me talk you out of this?"

"Nope."

"Fine." Kevin spat with finality. "I just hope you know what you're doing."

"I do."

But I didn't. I had no idea. That was sort of the point.

VIC-A-PALOOZA
May 16

Weekdays you could have the lake to yourself. That's the time to ski, when nobody else is around to muck up your sweet water. And if you caught an afternoon with no wind it was especially perfect. On those days the lake looked like glass and you could actually hear the water ripping beneath your skis. This particular Tuesday was one of those days and, like too many others, it was passing with me on my porch staring at it like a painting. A familiar sentiment entered my mind. "I'd be having a lot of fun right now if I wasn't alone."

By mid-May I'd discovered the major drawback to life among the unemployed - my friends still had jobs. I'd separated myself from the inmates, but it was hard to tell if I was free or in solitary confinement. It takes three people to water-ski legally. One to drive the boat, another to watch the skier. I couldn't even muster the driver. As I walked up town for lunch, I thought through the logic of trading my boat for a motorcycle.

At two o'clock, I entered Baby Boomers holding a realtor brochure. I slithered into my usual booth in the corner and waved to the waitress. Toni was a tall college student, summering at home with her parents. As usual, her blonde hair was pulled back in a ponytail. As she brought me my water, she pointed to a velvet Elvis painting and said, "Welcome to Planet Hollywood's hillbilly cousin."

Toni always made me laugh, and since I was bored anyway, I always went out of my way to strike up conversations. On this day, for lack of any legitimate subject matter, I asked who the hot bands were at Ball State.

She perked right up. "Why? Are you throwing a party?"

I'd never considered it before, but after seeing her enthusiasm, the idea sounded pretty good. "I've been sort of thinking about it."

"A big party?" she said, eyes wide at the thought.

"Of course a big party," I said, too caught up in the moment to think my answers through. "A big-ass Fourth of July bash."

Toni said, "Hold on. Let me put in your order and check my other table real quick." My rivals for her attention were four retired women playing euchre. Their weekly appearances demanded that Toni remain polite, but I could tell she was hurrying as she warmed up their coffee and asked if anyone wanted pie. Her relief when they declined was evident. Today, an extra nickel's tip couldn't compete with the excitement of party planning.

Toni returned with a pitcher of water. "I may have the perfect band for your party, but it depends," Toni said, as she refilled my glass.

"On?"

"On whether or not I'm invited."

"See, that's tough," I said. "I don't know you very well."

"I know who the best band is, but I'm not telling you unless I can come." She bit her bottom lip.

"We seem to be at a crossroads here," I said. "How about this? I hire the band now. If I get to know you better, you can come."

"Deal!" Toni said.

Summer suddenly became a lot more interesting.

Party plans were being formulated on the walk home. I had visions of all my friends together again, listening to a band and watching fireworks. Several boats anchored around my pier. I would call it "Vic-a-palooza."

The first to be invited was Kevin. "Sounds great," he said. "But I don't think you should have it on the Fourth. A lot of your friends have kids now, and they aren't going to dump them off at a babysitter's on a holiday. They're going to take them to the fireworks."

The date was moved. Not to the weekend before, but two weeks prior because, apparently, parents need a few weeks between major events. Next on my list was Wally Rourke. Before he got married we'd been inseparable. Afterwards? Well . . . let's just say there'd been some separation. And now his wife was pregnant. So in my mind this was probably going to be it for us. Once they had the baby I was pretty sure I'd be cut out entirely.

The concept of a party seemed to confuse Wally. "Why do you want to spend all the money on a band and stuff? Why not just have everyone bring a covered dish and listen to CDs?"

"Because that's not how a bachelor throws a bash!" What kind of lame-ass did he think I was? This wasn't a family reunion. It was Vic-a-palooza!

"Nobody cares. All the rest of us are married," Wally said.

"Don't remind me," I told him. "Now are you coming or not?"

He told me he would check with his wife and get back to me.

"Cut the engine," Toni ordered from the bow of my speedboat. She pointed to the green cottage in front of us. "I'm going to live there, for like a month, starting next Sunday."

"Really?" I asked. "Are your parents renting it or something?"

"Nope. I'm house sitting."

This was great news. She and I had hung out several times by now, but nothing was happening. We always had fun, but when the sun went down, Toni's highly controlling mom wanted her home. Perhaps now things would escalate.

Toni stepped to the bow of the boat and put her foot in the water. "Are we swimming or what?" She jumped in, and I followed. She splashed me. Then after I told her to stop she said, "What are you going to do about it?" That's when the wrestling began. She and I in 60 feet of water, our legs intertwined one moment, her backside pressed against my groin the next. I resisted enough to avoid defeat, but not so much that she would lose hope and abandon the fight.

After wearing ourselves out, she crawled up the stern of the boat and sat down on the ledge. Still floating in the lake, I held on to the ladder, looking up at the yellow two-piece clinging to her wet, tan body. Toni rubbed her foot down my arm slowly. I climbed the ladder and gently kissed her on the mouth.

She smiled and stepped into the boat. I followed her in, quickly wrapping a towel around my waist. We stretched out in the open bow, absorbing the last fleeting moments of sun. Toni laid her feet across my ankles.

"How old are you?" Toni asked.

I'd been fearing that question for weeks. "How old do you think I am?"

"You look about twenty-four or twenty-five," she said, examining my face. "But my mom says to own a house you must be older."

"You've discussed me with your mom?"

"Yeah, some of her friends wanted to know who I was spending so much time with."

"What's she think?"

"Honestly? She thinks you're some rich old perv trying to corrupt her daughter." Toni laughed.

"She said that?"

"In so many words, yeah."

"How old are you?" I asked.

"How old do you think I am?" She grinned playfully.

"Twenty-one or twenty-two, I suppose."

"I'm only twenty." She stopped making eye contact.

"Does that bother you? That I'm not twenty-one and all."

"No, I don't care. You're still the same person."

"That's good," she said, returning her gaze toward me. "How old are you?"

"Twenty-nine."

There was a pause. Toni moved her feet off of my legs and sat up. "Does that bother you?" I asked.

"I don't know. I really like you, but I know my mom wouldn't approve." She thought for a minute. "When's your birthday?"

"End of July."

Toni took a deep breath. "So really you're thirty."

"There's no need to rush it," I laughed.

"I don't know. I mean if you were like twenty-six even, it would be okay, but thirty. You know?"

"You thought I looked twenty-four. What makes the difference?"

"I don't know," she said. "Maybe it doesn't. I just need to think about it. I sort of wish you would've just lied."

SWEETIE
June 16

Wally and his pregnant wife, Stacy arrived the night before the party so we could catch up a little. For dinner we boated to one of the restaurants overlooking the lake. As we walked to my pier, the twenty or so geese in my yard waddled and honked toward the water, eventually taking flight.

"Holy shit! Where'd all those geese come from?" Wally asked.

"They live here," I told him. "They give me something to look at during the day."

"Do you feed them?" Stacy asked.

"No."

"Then why do they pick your yard?"

Most of the homes on Hamilton Lake had string stretched across their shoreline and other methods to keep the geese away. The birds were a nuisance. They ate my grass and left droppings all over my yard. But if there hadn't been a goose in my yard three months ago, I wouldn't have quit my job. I owed these geese a huge gratitude. It wouldn't be right to chase them away now.

"They seem sort of irritating to me," Wally said.

Ironically, the geese were far less irritating than Wally had become. "Are you warm enough, Sweetie?" he'd ask his wife. "Do you want to sit back here, Sweetie?" Stacy would comment on one of the houses. "Which one, Sweetie?" Sweetie. Sweetie. Sweetie.

When we arrived at the restaurant's dock Wally and Stacy stepped off the boat.

"Tie off the front end," I yelled. The order was not heard, or at least not heeded.

"Sweetie, do you want to go in and wait for us?" he asked. "I don't want you to get eaten up by mosquitoes."

While Wally and Sweetie discussed Sweetie's choice of standing outside or in, the boat was drifting away. Still aboard, I rushed over to the side and stuck my foot out to catch the pier. But the boat continued to drift, dragging my foot into the lake. Finally, after re-starting, backing out, and re-entering, I was able to tie it off.

Our dinner was not the pleasant experience I had hoped for either. My left foot was soaked, and Wally continued relentlessly with his barrage of "Sweeties."

"What are you going to eat, Sweetie? Do you want my seat so you can see the lake better, Sweetie?"

Stacy commented on missing the specials board when we walked in. Wally jumped out of his seat. "I'll go find out what they are, Sweetie."

That was finally all I could take. "Sit your ass down, Wally. The waitress will tell us what the specials are." I tried to smile, but things felt awkward. The rest of the dinner we made small talk about baby stuff. Nurseries and shit.

The next morning my alarm went off at six. The three of us were getting up early to ski before the lake got busy. By noon on Saturdays the lake was so crowded that skiing was both unpleasant and dangerous. But early in the morning it would be essentially vacant. I rolled out of bed, put on a swimsuit, walked down the hall and knocked on Wally's door.

"Wally," I whispered.

"Yeah," he whispered back.

"It's six, let's go."

"Okay," he said. "Give us ten minutes."

I walked to my pier to prepare the boat. It was so early that I passed the geese before they knew I was there. Like most speedboats on the lake, mine was stored on a lift, so I cranked the big round handle counter-clockwise until the boat was in the water. I reached in and turned on the blower. It wasn't particularly loud, but in the morning, when the lake is quiet, noise carries a long way.

On the walk back to the house the geese commenced with the customary honking and hissing. I made three trips from the garage to my boat carrying gear before returning to Wally's room. "Everything's loaded, let's go."

After starting the engine, I unraveled the ski rope and laid it out on the back. I arranged the life jackets and put on my wet suit and ski gloves.

I was slightly less than a mediocre skier, but I always looked good. Which actually means I looked silly, because having nice stuff and not being able to use it properly is a little ridiculous.

At ten till seven I marched back into the house and banged on Wally's door. "Come on, let's go."

"Give us ten minutes," he said again.

I went back out and shut off the engine. And for the next two hours I sat there alone, pissed. By nine there were 15 to 20 boats pulling skiers on the lake. It's an 800-acre lake, so there was still some room, but now the water was much rougher. At six my boat barely moved, now it rocked up and down, up and down. And it was getting worse by the minute. The public landing was crowded with boats and jet skis still waiting to unload. At 10:15, some jackass on a wave runner buzzed by on the wrong side of the "no wake" buoy and splashed me. The window for good skiing had officially passed.

At 11:10, Wally and Stacy finally appeared. "Ready," said Wally.

I said nothing. I was too angry to even make fun of his ratty old bathing suit with cartoon dogs. I turned on the blower, but this time it couldn't be heard over the scourge of watercraft assaulting the lake. After Wally checked to see where Sweetie wanted to sit, and if Sweetie was thirsty, he remembered they forgot their suntan lotion.

"Can you hold on a second?" Wally asked. "I need to run back into the house."

I backed away from the pier. "Go ahead and drive," I told Wally. "Get yourself used to the boat."

Wally took the wheel. Stacy sat in the bow and read some *What to Expect When You're Expecting* book. As soon as Wally felt comfortable driving, we stopped and I threw out the ski rope, my wake board, then jumped in myself. After strapping on the board, I signaled for Wally to slowly pull forward and tighten the rope. He misread my instructions and gunned it. I immediately let go to avoid having my arms pulled out of their sockets. Wally drove a little too far before noticing I wasn't up. Eventually he turned and came back.

"What happened?" he asked.

"Listen," I told him, yelling to be heard over the engine noise. "You have to pull forward slowly until the rope is taut, then take off."

"Right. Sorry, I'm a little rusty."

Wally circled the boat around me to return the rope. He crept forward to tighten it and made a very common mistake. By waiting too long to back off the throttle, he dragged me behind the boat. Struggling into position, I yelled, "Hit it."

He gunned it, and I was up. Things did not improve. Wally took off too fast, especially considering the turbulent water and heavy traffic. Eighteen miles an hour is my preferred speed on a wake board. He pulled me at 30. I gave him the standard "thumbs down" motion, hoping he'd nudge down the throttle a touch. But, making another common beginner's mistake, he slowed down too quickly, sinking me at about eight miles an hour. I gestured "thumbs up," and we were back to 30. In an act of surrender, I let go of the rope.

Wally didn't notice. He kept going. I went down at the northwest edge of the bay. Completely oblivious to my status, he reached the southwest corner and made the turn. I was pissed, because I could just imagine what was going on. Wally was pampering his wife. "Am I going too fast, Sweetie? Are you cold, Sweetie? Have you had enough, Sweetie?" Meanwhile alone and unprotected, I dodged speedboats and jet skis.

Hoping to make myself more visible, I released my feet from the wake board and held it vertically out of the water. As I watched Wally make the northeast turn I couldn't shut off the internal dialogue. "Are you having fun, Sweetie? Good book, Sweetie?" Wally continued along the northern edge of the lake. I waved at him, but he kept going straight.

An old man in a fishing boat perceived something was amiss and idled over to me. I recognized him because he fished the lake almost every day. He often brought a ten-year-old boy with him, just like my grandpa used to do with me when he was still alive. Occasionally, I watched them through binoculars. Seeing him help his grandson bait hooks brought tears to my eyes.

"Where's your boat?" he asked. I gestured with disgust to Wally now headed north on the far side of the bay. "What the hell's he doing over there?"

"I don't know," I said. "He's an idiot."

He stayed nearby in the chop protecting me from the other boats while Wally continued to go north, and continued and continued, ski rope bouncing off the water behind him.

"Where in the blazes is he going?" the old man asked. I turned my body 180 degrees to track his progress.

Wally turned the boat and headed west in a straight line. He was too far north to be coming toward me. He still didn't know I wasn't back there. He eventually hit the corner and turned south. As he completed his circle of the bay and once again drew closer, the old man and I screamed at him. He passed us, then looked back. I saw the puzzled expression on his face dissolve into shock as he realized what he had done.

As he slowly idled closer, the old man yelled at him. "What the hell do you think you're doing? This boy could have gotten killed out here!"

"I'm sorry," Wally said.

"Sorry wouldn't help your friend if he got hit by a boat."

"I know," Wally said, alternating his look of genuine chagrin with nervous, sideways glances at "Sweetie."

"You've got to pull your head out of your ass," the old man yelled.

His tirade relieved me of the responsibility of screaming at Wally in front of his wife, so I calmed down.

"All right. He screwed up," I said, climbing on to the boat. "Thank you very much, sir."

The old man drove off shaking his head. I removed my life jacket and Wally sheepishly gathered in the rope. Stacy sat in the bow, still reading her book.

"That was my fault," Wally whispered. "Stacy told me that you fell, and I misunderstood her."

I found it highly implausible that if she saw me fall she would only mention it once as he kept going. But we agreed on the main point. It was his fault. It was his responsibility to have her put down that stupid book and focus on the skier.

"Don't worry about it," I said. Those were the last words spoken until we got back to my pier.

"How can I help?" he asked, after I navigated the boat back into the lift.

"Never mind," I said, with no discernible tone. "Why don't you guys go uptown and have lunch or something."

"Aren't you coming?" he asked.

"Nah. I've got to wait around here for the tent people." I had rented a tent and tables for the party.

They climbed out of the boat and walked toward the house. The last thing I heard Wally say was, "Do you want to walk or drive, Sweetie?"

OLD TIMES
June 17

My friends arrived from three o'clock on, Kevin and Kylie the first among them. Kevin had appointed himself party bartender, which in this case meant filling up the igloo cooler with rum punch and making sure we always had beer flowing. While icing down the first keg, Kevin casually asked me what time Lauren was coming.

"I didn't invite her," I said.

"What!" he said. "You told me you were going to."

"I changed my mind. I'm trying to date another girl, and I was afraid it would be awkward."

Kevin threw a handful of ice into the plastic tub housing the keg. "Why must you constantly hurt me?"

"I'm sorry," I said. Kevin didn't comment. He just continued to throw ice into the tub. "Say something," I demanded.

"I'm very disappointed in you." Ignoring my laughter he continued, "I thought maybe Lauren would show up, looking all good. Then, perhaps after a few drinks, you guys would hook back up. Maybe start dating again."

"And that would make you happy, I suppose."

"I'd be happy for your happiness," he said.

"But she doesn't make me happy."

"That's because you have a self-destructive personality. God knows why, but you actually seem to prefer rejection and humiliation."

"That's not true," I said.

"It is true, or you'd still be dating Lauren." In his excitement, Kevin's voice had continued to rise, until it became loud enough for Kylie to hear.

She walked from the other side of the tent to join us. "Why are you yelling?"

"No reason," Kevin said, tapping the first keg. Kylie didn't buy it, so he finally told her about Lauren.

"Oh, let me guess. She's young and pretty?" Kylie said.

"Not as young as you're probably thinking," Kevin said nonchalantly, pouring a beer.

"And I suppose you planned on gawking at her in her bathing suit."

"No," Kevin lied to his wife. The red plastic cup in his hand was mostly foam, so he dumped it into the grass. Kylie still stared at him with narrowed eyes. If he didn't tell her the pathetic truth she would be angry the whole evening. Kevin exhaled a disgusted breath. He explained his vow of silence about my relationship with Lauren and how it tortured him. If we had gotten back together at this party, there'd be witnesses. He could've told everybody.

"Oh. I get it now," Kylie said. "And to think, I just thought you were a pervert."

"I'm not a pervert," Kevin said. "I'm a gossip. You know that."

My caterer, "Fat Stevie's Ribs" served dinner at seven. I didn't get a chance to eat because I was too busy mingling with my guests, who essentially divided themselves into two sections. Old college buddies in one cluster, local friends in another. By eight o'clock the attendance had swelled passed 70. But the guest I had most wanted to entertain was still a no-show. During the weeks leading up to my party, Toni and I continued to see each other platonically.

Toni and six of her friends finally arrived around 8:20, ten minutes before The Moody McCarthy band was supposed to start. But by 8:40, The Moody McCarthy band, which consisted of its namesake on an acoustical guitar, had not arrived, making me very tense. I reassured Toni that he was probably just lost or something, but she cast me a suspicious look. She probably wanted to impress her friends as much as I wanted to impress her, and Moody was making us both look stupid.

At 8:50, Moody rolled in with his van. He was a decent-looking guy with dark hair and a big salesman type smile. He wore old cut-off jean shorts and a Hawaiian shirt. He never told anyone his age, but you can usually tell if someone is about your own age or not, and Moody was approximately mine. By 9:10 he was playing and the party took off. My guests, many already drunk, were dancing. I could smell marijuana. A couple would eventually be caught naked in the neighbor's yard. It felt like old times again. I was happy.

At 10:30 Toni approached me. "This is a great party! I still can't believe Moody McCarthy is here!"

I asked Toni if she wanted to "take a break" with me in the house.
"I don't know," she said. "My friends."

Her friends, being ogled by my friends, were busy dancing and trying
to be noticed by Moody. "They'll be fine," I said.

"All right, but just for a minute." We entered my house and sat down
on the couch. I put my arm around her. Toni didn't move. She stared at
the television, which wasn't on. I kissed her lightly on the cheek. She did-
n't react. I kissed her on the forehead. Again nothing. It was like she was
an inmate, begrudgingly accepting something horrible to survive prison.

"You know what, Toni?" I said. "You clearly don't want to be with
me. And that's fine. I still like you a lot as a person. I'm just not going to
try to date you anymore." I stood up to go back outside.

Toni grabbed my arm. "Wait," she said. "I don't want you to give
up." She stared down at her feet. Through the window we could hear the
partygoers cheer as Moody finished a cover of "Cheeseburger in
Paradise."

"What do you want me to do?"

"This," Toni said, and put her left hand on the back of my head and
kissed me. It began as a little kiss, but quickly grew in confidence and
passion and showed no signs of letting up. It might have built to something significant, had Wally and Stacy not come barging in.

"Whoops," Wally said. "Sorry to interrupt."

Toni jumped up. "I have to go find my friends." She ran back outside.

"We're taking off," Wally said. I hadn't really spoken to him since the
lake incident, but it still kind of hurt my feelings. He and Stacy both
assured me they had a great time, but since Stacy was pregnant, she
became tired much easier.

Apparently, it wasn't just like old times.

By midnight a seedier crowd crept in, mostly townies whom I'd never
met before. I didn't say much, other than to mention if they wanted beer,
and of course they did, they had to pay. They coughed up some cash.
Not enough really, but I let it slide. That's when I knew I was throwing a
great party. My friends were acting like drunken assholes, and drunken
assholes were trying to act like they were my friends.

At three I looked around. Of the 25 people still standing, less than half had actually been invited. When the eighth keg went dry, Kevin asked if he should crack open the cases of beer I had stored in my house. I told him, "Absolutely not." Moody finished his set, and the crashers left.

As I paid Moody, he asked if I could hook him up with a place to spend the night. I wanted to help him, but I had no room. Every bed, couch, and open space on the floor was already filled by my guests. I spotted Toni and her friends hanging around hoping to meet Moody. "Hey Toni, do you have any room at your cottage?"

"Why?" she asked suspiciously, looking around. Many of my friends were still stumbling around.

"Moody needs a place to stay and I don't have any room."

Toni brightened immediately. Her friends all squealed with delight. Moody made his plans with Toni, and I walked around my house to make sure nothing was amiss. I was disappointed that I wouldn't be spending the night with Toni, but was fairly certain I'd laid the ground-work.

I struggled out of bed at 11:30 the next morning. Most everyone had taken off. As I walked to my refrigerator I noticed several notes on the counter and some cash. People congratulating me on a good party and saying their good-byes.

Outside, I squinted in the bright sun and inspected the damage. Moody's van was still parked in my yard, protecting the only patch of grass that had not been destroyed from the wild frenzy of dancing. There were paper cups and bottles scattered everywhere. The worst were the cigarettes. All night people had smoked and carelessly thrown their butts on my lawn. The geese were back, and they honked angrily at me.

I grabbed a trash bag and gathered the debris. It was a daunting project, and my mind drifted from the menial work to the bigger picture. I had thrown a great party. Everyone had loved it and would talk about it for years to come. Yet, right at that moment, I was alone, raking up after people who didn't care enough about me to use a trash can.

A little after noon, Toni dropped off Moody. I waved her into the yard but, apparently not seeing me, she drove off.

"Man, that was a great party you had last night," Moody said, as he unlocked his van.

"Thanks," I said, no longer really caring. "How was everything over at Toni's? Did she take care of you?"

Moody smiled sheepishly.

"What?" I asked.

"Yeah," Moody chuckled. "She took care of me."

I kicked a plastic garbage can half way across my yard, spilling the trash I had spent all morning raking up.

"You don't have anything going with her, do you?" Moody asked.

"I did, but not anymore," I said.

"Are you sure?"

"I'm sure."

Moody was relieved. "That would have been horrible."

Changing the subject, I said, "Hey, do you know anything about motorcycles? I'm thinking about getting one."

GETTING OUT EASY
June 23

Six days after my party, I sat in an inner tube 50 feet from shore, paddling in circles. I was trying to see how fast I had to spin myself before the tube would give me four "hands free" rotations. I should've been mowing my yard or something productive, but I was too bored to stop. Plus it was hot, and being in the lake felt good. So I spun in circles thinking about what was next in my life. Allowing my desires to lead me to my destiny was still the plan. But currently I didn't desire to do much of anything, which was unsettling.

"Working on your tan?" Standing in my yard was a middle-aged man with curly brown hair. He'd been at my house earlier that week, wearing the same green gingham shirt. It draped across his broad shoulders unbuttoned, giving the world a view of his gray chest hair and medicine ball stomach. "You had any other offers on your house this week?" he yelled.

The day after the party I placed a "For Sale by Owner" sign in my front yard. I doubted anything would happen, but I decided to give it to the end of summer before I signed with a realtor. This guy showed up two days later in a silver BMW with Florida plates.

Touring the house, he turned on every faucet and flushed each toilet twice. After taking down several notes, mostly name brands and ages of the appliances, he offered me exactly what I had paid for the place. Exactly. I refused. He left his number in case I changed my mind. I tossed it the moment he left, and hadn't given him a second thought.

He walked to the end of my pier so he could stop yelling across the lake. "You thought about my offer?"

"No," I said, paddling further away. He gave off a crooked car salesman vibe. I didn't trust him.

"Seriously. What do you want for this place?"

"I don't know. I haven't really thought about it." Why give him a price to negotiate down from? If he was interested he could give me a price and I would negotiate up.

He laughed. "I can see you're a man who doesn't like bullshit. Let's cut right to it then. We both know that your house is worth around two hundred. We both know you paid one-eighty. Now if you list it through a realtor you could net one-ninety after commissions and costs, but you might not get that for several months."

"Maybe," I said. I didn't want to tip my hand, but he was exactly right. Plus, what he didn't mention was my huge mortgage. Most of my bonus had been spent on buying a car. I had come close to over-extending myself on this place when I had a job. Now I would have to liquidate stocks to be able to make my house payments for the next year. I paddled closer.

"When you do sell your house," he continued, "there's a pretty good chance the buyers will already have their own furniture. That could mean another couple thousand dollars on movers and storage for your stuff."

Not to mention the huge pain in the ass, I thought.

"I'll tell you what I'll do. I'll give you one-ninety-two for everything." He waved a piece of paper at me. I paddled to the pier. It was an official offer, with an itemized list. When he said everything, he damn near meant it. The list included my furniture, the appliances, my bar, the plates and silverware, the mounted fish, the lawnmower, the gas grill, and the television.

Now I didn't know how much my furnishings were worth exactly, but I was pretty sure it was more than $2,000. "I think the house with all of those furnishings is worth two-fifteen. Easy," I said, handing it back to him.

"Well, you're right and you're wrong," he said with a sleazy smile. "It might be worth two-fifteen, but getting it ain't gonna be easy. If you want easy, and I'm guessing that you might, it's worth one-ninety-two and not a penny more. At least, to me."

The only desire I currently had was to buy a motorcycle, and I couldn't afford one until I sold my boat. I wasn't doing that while I still lived on the lake. This offer might've been the only one I'd get before next spring, but I wanted a better price. My negotiating technique was silence. If you're quiet long enough, sometimes the other person gets uncomfortable and offers a little more. I paddled in circles for five minutes and he didn't speak up once. Finally, I had enough, "One-ninety-five."

"One-ninety-two is final."

"Fuck it. Why not?"

A week later his check cleared, my boat sold, and I walked away from my old life. Some people would say that was the moment I became a free man, open to all of life's offerings. No debts, responsibilities, or commitments to impede my journey. Living as God and nature had intended. That's how I saw it.

Others would argue that I was 30, a man with no wife, no job, and living with my parents. That's how my mom saw it.

BACK HOME
July 5

For the longest time, my mother's only comment on my recent life change was, "I don't like it, but you're an adult. I can't say anything." That policy changed radically the day I moved back home.

The tribunals took place each night at dinner. Tonight would be session number four. "So you're not even going to look for another job?" Mom asked, pouring drinks at the kitchen counter. I hadn't even sat down yet.

"I just quit my last one. Why would I want another?"

She forcefully exhaled from her nose. "This is the craziest thing I've ever heard of." Coming from a long line of worriers, Mom wasn't dealing well with this "blatant irresponsibility."

My dad stepped in from outdoors carrying a plate of grilled steaks. Molly, their black and tan Welsh Corgi followed him in. I smacked my hands on my thighs until she jumped up and gave me a hug.

Mom carried the drinks to the table and sat down. "What are you going to do for money? Your father and I aren't going to give you any. Are we Ray?"

Dad shrugged his shoulders. He had doubts about my decision too, but accepted the fact that it was already made.

"I've got money," I told her. "I just sold my house."

"We'll just see how long that lasts."

Everyone forked a steak to their plate, and we passed the potatoes. Dad took a bite of his steak. "Man, this is good. This is better than any steak I've ever gotten at a restaurant. What do you think, Karen?"

She ignored him. Her focus was still on me. "You just think you're going to live here, rent free, I suppose."

"Do you want me to pay rent?"

After a pause, she said, "No. I suppose not."

"Then what are you complaining about? I'm not going to live here forever. Just until I figure out what to do next."

"She just wants to bitch," was Dad's take on the exchange.

Molly barked, and Mom threw her a little piece of steak.

"Hey, God damn it," Dad said. "Don't do that."

"What *are* you going to do next?" Mom asked me.

"I don't know."

"What do you mean, you don't know? Why'd you quit your job, then?"

"I didn't like it."

"You made tons of money, a company car, fancy trips. It sounds horrible." Mom worked at a paper products factory. "Your father and I hated most of our jobs, but we didn't quit. Did we Ray?"

"I would've loved to," he said, scooping more potatoes.

"Your dad's as lazy as you are," Mom huffed.

Dad took offense. "What are you talking about? I've worked my entire life."

"You know you'd rather sit in the basement and watch TV."

"No shit," he said. "But I don't."

"That's because I stay on you." Dad waved her off and went back to work on his steak. "Tell me," Mom said, turning her nagging back to me. "You've got to have some idea what you're going to do."

"Do you really want to know?" I asked.

"Yes."

"All right then. I'm buying a motorcycle."

"You're going to kill yourself," was Mom's knee-jerk reaction.

I was prepared for this argument. "What about you and your horses?" Mom and Dad each owned a horse they went for trail rides on. "They're just as dangerous."

"Now you're just being stupid," she said.

"Am I? Ever since Christopher Reeve, I've been worried sick about you." Dad laughed. "But do you care?" I carried on, teasing my mom. "Will you give up the horses, so I can sleep at night? No. Now you'll know how I feel."

Molly barked for more steak. Dad pointed at Mom. "Don't even think about it."

Mom threw Molly a piece of fat anyhow. "That's it then," she said to me. "You're going to buy a motorcycle and what, just ride around all day?"

"Basically, until it gets too cold to ride, then I'm going to backpack through Europe."

"Oh, for Pete's sake." This was too much for her. Traveling to my mother was a complete waste of money. In the end, you'd have nothing to show for it. The few trips she had taken were to see relatives. The concept of actually paying for a hotel room was as foreign to her as a Rabbi taking communion.

"How long are you going to stay in Europe?" Dad asked.

"Until I decide to come home."

"That's ridiculous," Mom said.

"Why?"

"Because you don't have a job!" She dropped her fork onto the plate. "Unemployed people do not buy motorcycles and travel through Europe."

Molly reacted to my mom with several loud barks. Dad said, "Settle down."

"Don't tell me to settle down," Mom yelled. "Your son has decided to become a...uh...hippie. That doesn't bother you?"

Dad and I both laughed.

"You think it was hard finding a wife when you owned a house and had a job. Try now, unemployed and living with your parents."

"I'm going to tell people that I'm rich and you guys are my servants."

Mom stood up. "I'm never going to have grandchildren."

"You should have had more kids," I told her. "It would have helped your odds."

"Who would have ever known you were going to be this screwed up?" Mom exited to the barn, Molly right behind her.

Even though I had seemingly laughed off her concerns, she had succeeded in planting the seeds of doubt. Women probably would find me pathetic. Maybe I never would get married and have kids.

Dad, already finished with his meal, eyed Mom's mostly untouched steak. "You want part of that?"

"Nah," I said, too nervous to eat. "Go ahead."

LOOKING THROUGH THE TURN
July 13

I was polishing the chrome on my motorcycle when a bigger bike barreled past my house, slammed on its brakes, and rolled into my parents' yard. The driver was a big son of a bitch, nearly 300 pounds, with a gray, bushy beard.

I had scheduled a private motorcycle safety instructor for the day. This was either him or I was about to be pummeled. "You Roger?"

"Yep," he said, straddling his bike. His enormous, sunburned gut hung out of his black Sturgis T-shirt. "Call me Puff." Puff removed his sunglasses and wiped the sweat off his face with the sleeve of his T-shirt.

Between the black denim of Puff's thighs stood a masterpiece of motorcycle art. The gas tank was jet black with a ferocious green dragon's head blowing orange flames. The front fender sported the dragon's forearms, with lethal claws poised to strike. A thrashing tail and powerful hindquarters were painted on the rear fender. The exhaust pipe and engine coverings had small feathery etchings, making the side of his bike look like magnificent chrome wings.

"That is one sweet ride," I told him.

He patted the gas tank like it was a horse's neck. "I thank ya." He glanced down at my Honda Shadow. "You got a nice-looking bike, too."

Him saying that about my bike was so absurd I laughed out loud. It did look nice, but it wasn't altered one bit from the factory floor. But the meaning of his compliment wasn't lost on me. It was one of two typical responses from Harley guys when they find out you ride anything but a Harley. They either say, "It's just important that you ride," or utter a dismissive snort followed by "Pussy." Puff was letting me know that he wasn't here to judge. Actually, besides his grizzly appearance there was nothing threatening about him. He was a man who could be looked straight in the eye without feeling challenged.

"Now what's the problem you're having, exactly?" he asked me.

"I can't turn."

He laughed. "That is a problem."

It was a huge problem, and I wasn't exaggerating. The first hour of owning my bike, I stopped at an intersection and revved the engine to show off to a geeky 12-year-old mowing his grass. With a big, goofy smile, the kid gave me a thumbs-up. I raised my right fist in triumph, let out the clutch, and screwed up the turn so badly that the bike fell on top of me in his yard.

After getting home, I spent the rest of the week too frightened to venture past my country block. All day, driving in circles, first one direction, then the other, stopping at each turn and pushing the bike with my feet. At one point, our smart-ass neighbor yelled, "Did you forget something?"

"Jump on your bike and let me watch you ride," Puff said.

I started my bike, put on my helmet and slowly rolled out onto the quiet road. Puff followed. My bike was in third gear when I hit the first corner. I downshifted to second and attempted the left turn. Failing, I hit the brakes and stopped before I went into the ditch.

Puff said something to me, but I couldn't hear him over The Dragon's loud pipes. He shut off his engine and repeated. "You're too worried about making the turn."

"That's because I keep landing in the ditch," I told him.

"That's because you're thinking about the ditch," he replied.

I wanted to say, "No shit," but didn't.

"See, when you make the turn you're looking at the ditch. That's why you end up there. You have to look through your turn."

"Look through the turn?" I didn't get it.

"When you turn, look at where you want to end up and your body will naturally do what it needs to do to get you there. Whatever you focus on is where you're going wind up."

On the next turn I looked up the road and the bike followed my eyes. "Good," Roger said, "now, as long as there aren't any vehicles coming, I want you to weave in and out of the dotted yellow lines. Each time looking through your turn."

Quickly I gained confidence and increased speed. At the corner, eyes up ahead, my body naturally steered the bike. I wasn't even conscious of my arms turning the handlebars. The next road was busier so I couldn't do any weaving, but another flawless left turn brought me back home. Soon I was doing figure eight's and U-turns. In less than an hour, Puff had cured me.

"What do I owe you?" I asked, willing to pay almost anything in my current state of bliss.

"Case of beer," Puff replied.

"Don't you want some money?"

"Nah," Puff said. "But I don't want no cheap shit. I want Coors Light."

I tried to protest, but Puff interrupted. "Not everything in life has to be about money, does it?"

"No, I don't suppose. I just want to properly thank you. It might not seem like it to you, but what you helped me do today is a big deal. A really big deal."

"Oh. In that case I want some beer *and* a pizza."

We finished the afternoon by soaking up the sun in the parking lot of the local Domino's, splitting a pepperoni pizza and talking motorcycles.

"This will sound kind of stupid," I said, "but I quit a pretty good job to be able to just kind of do this for a while. And when I couldn't ride my bike, I was uh, you know."

"Shittin' your pants?" Puff put the finishing touches on yet another Coors Light.

"Yeah, sort of," I replied, drinking Coke.

"I don't think that's stupid at all," he said. "Hell, I was a corporate CPA for seventeen years."

Surely he was yanking my chain. "You were an accountant?"

"Still am, sort of." He worked tax season preparing personal tax returns. He also kept the books for a local Harley dealer in exchange for parts and merchandise.

"That's cool. People keep telling me I'm crazy."

Puff opened another beer. "People told me the same crap. Who says we have to judge success the same way those miserable bastards do?"

"Still, it does make me a little nervous."

"What do you really want in life, money or happiness?"

"Happiness, of course," I said. "But I'm not really sure at this point, what would make me happy."

"You won't, until you get to know yourself. And you can't do that when you spend all your time working. If you have a job, then you'll be that job. You'll never know who you really are."

There was one slice of pizza left, which Puff gulped down in three big bites. With his mouth still full, he said, "Riding's going to be good for you."

"It should be fun."

"It'll be that, but there's more to it. When you ride a bike there aren't any radios or cell phones. It's just you alone with your thoughts. It's a beautiful thing. Knees in the breeze and bugs in your teeth."

It was funny to watch this big biker wax poetic. "I think you missed your calling. You should have been a priest or something."

"Priests can't marry," Puff said.

"You're married?" I asked. He wasn't wearing a ring, or probably more telling, a watch.

"Not anymore. My wife dumped my ass when I quit my job."

"Thank you for confirming my worst fears."

Puff laughed. "You're going be all right, kid." He started The Dragon. Over the "um, um, um, um" rumbling of the engine, he shouted, "Don't forget now, look through your turns."

My motorcycle safety instructor then rode his motorcycle onto Auburn's busiest street, buzzed on beer and not wearing a helmet.

DENNY
July 27

The Fort Wayne Wizards are a triple-A baseball team in the San Diego Padres farm system. I have no idea how many years they've been in Fort Wayne. I remember when they weren't around, so it couldn't have been too long. They never crossed my mind. Ever. Then one day, out of nowhere, I suddenly had an urge to check out a game.

I was on one of my now daily motorcycle excursions. Without any predisposed destination, I rode my motorcycle aimlessly to see where I'd end up. That day, like too many prior, I seemed to drift into my old sales territory. This unnerved me. I had to think of someplace else to go quickly before the depression set in. Passing a park, I watched boys playing baseball and thought, "The Wizards."

It occurred to me on the 45 minute ride to Fort Wayne that the Wizards might not have a home game that day. And it also occurred to me if they did, it might not be until the evening. It didn't matter. I didn't want to see a baseball game. I wanted to ride my motorcycle to a specific destination that wasn't part of my past.

I lucked out. The Wizards closed out a five-game home stand that afternoon. Working the ticket counter was a middle-aged woman trying to conceal the fact she was smoking. "How many you needin'?" she asked in a deep, gravely voice.

"Just one," I said.

"Just one," she repeated. "You's in luck. You can get a seat behind the Wizards' dug-out."

"Sounds good," I said, handing her a five.

"They's always lots of good seats that sits empty just because they's singles and most people come in a group."

"Lucky me."

For 30 minutes I sat alone, comfortably eating hotdogs in the sun. I enjoyed the fact that no one occupied the three seats to my left and hoped it would stay like that all afternoon. But it wasn't meant to be.

Moments before the game started, an obese man waddled in my direction. He was round and lumpy like a boulder and sported a homemade baseball uniform. Backwards ball cap, huge, untucked Wizards jersey to cover his massive girth, black sweat pants cut off at mid calf, white socks pulled up, and black tennis shoes. The audience cheered his arrival and he waved his hat to show appreciation.

"It looks like you're a celebrity around here," I said, as he sat down beside me.

"A little bit," he chuckled. The Wizards' pitcher, Andy "Fastball" Vastola took the mound. "Come on, Fastball!" he yelled.

Fastball walked the leadoff batter. The blubbery body next to me tensed up. "Darn it, Fastball." His voice was high to begin with, but when he got angry his pitch rose to a cartoonish magnitude. A snack vendor walked by and handed the man two hotdogs. He hadn't asked for them and I didn't see him pay. Fastball then struck out the next three batters. As he walked back from the mound my row mate stood up and faced the crowd. He raised his hands in the air like it was a rock concert and chanted, "Fastball...Fastball...Fastball..."

The big man already smelled from perspiration, and I saw no hope that things would improve as the day wore on. Hoping to exit his company gracefully, I commented on all of the empty seats in the outfield.

"Most people are at work," he said. "Night games draw more."

I stood up to leave. "That makes sense. I think I'm-"

"Why aren't you at work?"

"I don't have a job." This felt awkward. If I left now it might look like I was embarrassed about being unemployed. I sat back down. "I'm taking time off to experience life for a while."

His eyes lit up. "For as long as possible, live free and uncommitted. It makes little difference if you are committed to jail or the family farm."

"Right on. That's a good one," I said.

He replied, "Thoreau," but I thought he said "throw". I turned my attention back to the field. "Henry David Thoreau," he continued. "That's his quote."

The leadoff batter for the Wizards, Tommy Squires, jumped on the first pitch and it looked like it was gone. The clammy stranger waved his hands as if he could fan the ball and shouted, "Go! Go!" When it was caught on the warning track he slapped his thigh, "Crap!"

He turned back to me. "You ever read *Walden* or *Self-Reliance* by Emerson?"

"Uh, no. Are they good?"

"Yeah," he said, like *I* was the idiot. "They're pretty good."

"Maybe I'll check them out sometime then," I said, more eager to escape now than ever. I had no desire to let this fat sumbitch ridicule me for nine innings.

After yelling at the umpire for calling a bad strike, the fat man turned back to me and said, "I think anybody who quits his job to enjoy life, might relate with the themes. Not longing for more than you need. Appreciating the beauty of nature. Enjoying the simple pleasures."

That caught my attention. "Actually, I do think I'd enjoy that."

"I figured you would when you responded to the quote."

Curious now, I asked this baby-faced man what his deal was. It took him over six innings to answer that question. His name was Denny. He was a 28-year-old transcendentalist who lived with his mother in New Haven. He didn't care about possessions or appearance. He only sought wisdom. His life's work was writing important social essays.

"Have you studied Buddhism?" he asked. I hadn't. "I wrote an essay on it once. When you see how many ways Buddhism actually agrees with Christianity you learn that there is only one truth, one wisdom, and that is the closest evidence I have to proving there's a God or life force."

He made the finger quotation marks when he said, "life force."

"But people focus on the differences, which is generally the stuff no one can prove. Apparently, a soul being reincarnated into another being is ridiculous when you compare it to your soul ascending into a world of clouds somewhere behind a set of pearly gates."

"That does sound interesting," I said.

"It's great." Denny was presumably talking about Buddhism in general and not his own essay, although it was hard to tell with him. "The beginner's mind. The four noble truths. If you want to progress you need to know about this stuff."

Just then, with runners on first and second and no outs, Wizards' shortstop Scott Burton grounded into a double play, advancing the runner to third. It was the bottom of the sixth and the Wizards were down three runs to zip.

"Darn it!" Denny said. He stood up and stretched his legs by grabbing an ankle and pulling it up to his butt. An excited buzz came over the crowd. I could hear people laughing, but it didn't really seem like they were making fun of him. Left fielder Andy Miller popped out to shallow right, and the inning was over.

Denny marched straight toward the field. For a moment I thought he was going to assault the players. But instead he climbed atop the Wizards' dugout and faced the cheering crowd. Over the stadium sound system the rap song "Baby Got Back," by Sir Mix-a-Lot began.

Denny's dancing was a combination of all styles popular in the past 30 years. There was the running man from the late '80's. Some disco from the '70's. With a lot of hip-hop and breakdancing thrown in. The small crowd of regulars loved it. Children danced in front of their seats. People were clapping. A group of fans yelled, "Go Denny. Go Denny." And he did. He went like hell. Doing something that resembled a man jumping rope and hula-hooping at the same time. Finally the song ended. Denny took a bow.

After returning to his seat, Denny said, "I was thinking. You should definitely get a book on the four noble truths." He was wiping the sweat off his face and neck with a towel thrown to him by a player. His face was bright red, and he struggled to catch his breath.

"Are you gonna be okay?" I asked.

"I'm fine," he said. A drink vendor walked by and handed him a large Mountain Dew. Denny took a large swig. Then a deep breath and finally another drink. Returning to thoughts of my spiritual guidance he said, "Now there are a lot of books on the four noble truths. I like the one by the Dalai Lama for you because it's so basic."

"Are you the official team mascot?" I asked.

"Of course not," Denny said, offended. "I'm a dancer."

I laughed really, really hard.

Denny raised his eyebrows at me with a quiet indignation. "I dance for the Wizards in baseball and the Komets in hockey. They each pay me twenty-five hundred a season and free food at the games. That makes me a professional dancer."

"Okay."

"Since I live with my mother and have little use for material things, five-thousand is plenty for me to live on. And it frees up most of my time for writing. Like my current thing." Denny rubbed his hands together excitedly. He was writing an essay on why the Martin Luther King Jr. holiday should be more appreciated by whites.

"It would have been very easy for King to lead with hatred and anger," he said. "Then we would have had one heck of a mess. Instead, he taught love and humanity. We should respect that more as a country."

It was the top of the ninth inning. The Wizards were still down three. Denny was telling me the importance of meditation in finding one's spiritual essence. When the relief pitcher for the Wizards retired the side, Denny said, "The team needs me now."

He rose from his seat, raised both arms in the air like a football referee when someone kicks a field goal, and chanted. Three beats. "Wizards" *clap*. "Wiz-ards" *clap*. Pretty soon the crowd was into it. ""Wizards" *clap*. "Wiz-ards" *clap*. And the Wizards, despite Denny's cheers, went three up and three down, losing the game.

"Dog gone it," Denny said. "Why do I even try?"

BLIND DATE
July 29

I was browsing through the spirituality section when a blonde woman entered the bookstore and bee-lined it to the magazine rack. After three false alarms, one regrettably and two thankfully, it appeared my blind date had arrived. She looked nervous. Was she afraid I wouldn't like her or that she wouldn't like me? You may feel anxiety over both, but one usually weighs heavier. In my case, it was neither since I didn't want to go on this stupid date in the first place.

I'd been bullied into it on my 30th birthday. I was in a bad mood because 30 just kind of does that to you. Mom didn't make it any better. "I'll never have grandkids. All your friends are married and having kids. Why can't you?" In an effort to get her off my back, my aunt mentioned a girl from her church that would be just perfect for me. She was 26, college educated, and had just broken up with her fiancé.

When asked about what we would have in common my aunt said "tons" but never really landed on anything specific.

Mom said, "You're both single. That's enough." Just as I was about to reject this entire thing, my uncle mentioned that she was really good looking. My aunt upgraded her condition to beautiful.

"Now why wouldn't you go out with her?" Mom demanded to know.

"Fine," I said. "If it'll shut you up, I'll go out with her."

I approached the blonde at the magazine rack. Her fingers flipped through a magazine, but her eyes scanned the bookstore for someone who met my description, only probably a little better looking. "Stephanie?" I asked.

She looked neither pleased nor horrified, which was about how I felt. She wasn't beautiful as promised, but she definitely wasn't ugly either. She could have been real attractive if her hair and fashion weren't so outdated.

Standing in line at the register, she grabbed my wrist and lifted my arm to see the books I was purchasing. Thoreau's *Walden* and a book on Buddhism, which she immediately wrinkled her nose at. "Buddhism, huh?"

"It's really interesting," I told her, trying to ignore her condescending tone. "The four noble truths and whatnot."

"I see," she said.

She insisted on driving instead of riding my motorcycle, even though I'd brought an extra helmet. Seconds after we pulled out of her parking spot, she slammed the brakes of her Ford Mustang. A man with a car load of kids cut us off. Stephanie took this as a hostile act and immediately retaliated by slamming the gas pedal. We accelerated within inches of its rear bumper. The driver refused to acknowledge. She rode his ass all the way out of the parking lot. I hated this girl, and we hadn't even had dinner yet.

Things got worse at the Red Lobster. When our salads arrived, I made my standard first-date joke. I lifted my right hand for her to grab and said, "Would you mind leading us in prayer?" Usually the girl makes a terrified look, I tell her I'm just kidding and we share a laugh. Not this time. She grabbed my hand, closed her eyes, and prayed. And not just a short little memorized prayer we Catholics fire off in about three seconds. This was one of those love letters to Jesus kind of prayers. An "Oh Jesus, we are just so thankful for all you have given us and it's such a beautiful day that reflects your glory..." kind of ordeal that goes on and on. Plus, she raised her free hand into the air. Utterly humiliating. I caught a waitress staring at us out of the corner of my wide-open eyes. I made the crazy signal by circling my left index finger around my ear. The waitress nodded her agreement.

"That was nice," Stephanie said, quite proud of herself. "When I saw you buying that Buddhism book I was a little nervous. As a Christian I feel there is only one truth," she said. Then added, "Jesus," in case the term Christian wasn't clear enough.

Stephanie would get no arguments from me. I knew this was my fault. "I've been to your church a few times," I told her, while buttering a cheddar biscuit. "It's nice."

"My whole family goes there. My parents, my aunts and uncles. Everybody but my one cousin."

"Why? Did he marry a Catholic?"

"No. He's gay," she said.

I waited for the waitress to refill our drinks before I said, "That's too bad about your cousin and all."

"Yeah, his parents were really upset."

"No, I meant that he doesn't feel comfortable at your church," I clarified. "It's fine that he's gay."

"No, it's not," she said. "Even the Bible says it's wrong."

"Where in the Gospel does it say you can't be gay?"

She named something in the Old Testament.

"I only accept John, Matthew, Luke or…" I couldn't think of Mark. "You know, the four Gospels. The rest is pretty shady if you ask me."

"You think the rest of the Bible is shady?" She was horrified.

"Well, not shady, just inconsistent. It's full of wisdom, and I really like a lot of it. I just don't think you're supposed to take the Old Testament literally."

She pushed away her salad bowl. She had completely stopped eating at this point. I, on the other hand, grazed happily. "You don't believe in the Old Testament?" she asked.

"I don't think you can say it's wrong to be gay just because the Old Testament says so. If that were the case, then I could have slaves to wait on my ten wives."

"That's not the same thing," she said.

"Fine. Let's talk about something from the Old Testament that we both agree on. Adam and Eve. Now you don't think that at one point there were just those two people, right?"

"Yes," said Stephanie, "I believe in Creation."

"Even with all of the discoveries of pre-historic man?"

"If you don't believe in the Bible then you're not a Christian!"

"No, I believe in the Gospel. All you've proven is that I'm not Jewish."

Our waitress arrived with our main courses. She placed my crab legs in front of Stephanie, but I corrected her before the chicken entrée could hit the table. I should have taken this opportunity to change the subject, but I was curious.

"What do you think the story of Adam and Eve represents?" I asked, breaking a crab leg in half.

"How man was created," she said.

"That's all?" I pressed. "No message outside of that?"

"Well, and to follow God's commands."

"Which are?" I asked with a mouth full of delicious crab.

"In this case, not to eat the apple."

"Or maybe just to live a simple life," I suggested.

"What?"

"Look at it. They're in paradise. Enjoying all the food and drink they need, unaware of personal possessions. Then they eat from the apple of knowledge and realize they're naked. They get kicked out of paradise and from then on life becomes a big hassle of fashion, property, and exerting one's wealth. God didn't make our lives complicated. We did." I cracked open another crab leg and dipped it in hot butter.

The waitress came to our table and looked at Stephanie's plate of untouched food. "Is everything okay?" she asked.

"The *food's* fine," Stephanie said.

It amazed me how upset she was getting. I have no credibility on the subject. Who cares what I think? But Stephanie looked like she might cry... or scream. Either would have been uncomfortable. "I'm sorry," I told her. "You're probably right about all of that stuff."

The rest of our dinner was spent talking about Indiana versus Purdue in basketball. An equally touchy matter in this state, but much more easily proven through statistics. When the check came she demanded to pay for her own dinner. I offered some polite resistance, but when she insisted I let her. I asked if she wanted to pay for mine as well. She did not.

There was no discussion about exchanging phone numbers or seeing each other again when she returned me to the bookstore. Stephanie did have one question for me. Did I really believe all those things I said?

"I don't know," I told her. "I have kind of an odd moral code. I think you can do anything you want as long as it doesn't hurt other people. Drinking. Sex. Cussing. Who cares? As long as it doesn't interfere with somebody else's happiness, then more power to you."

"You realize that you can't get into Heaven by good deeds. You have to accept Christ. It says so right in the Bible."

It also says Jesus didn't start preaching until he was 30. I wish more young Christians would quote that, then shut their condescending mouths.

"Yeah, I know," I said.

Stephanie had an odd look on her face.

"What? I accept Jesus."

"Not if you're still sinning."

Good deeds can't get me into Heaven, but bad deeds come back to bite me in the ass. This deal just keeps getting worse and worse. "I'm going to stop."

"Stop what?"

"Sinning. You know drinking, cussing, having sex."

"I'll pray for you," she said.

"Well then, I guess I've got that going for me."

ASHLEY

July 29

As the motorcycle gently idled between my legs, I pulled the crash helmet down over my ears. It was only 8:03 and my date had already ended. Fifty-eight minutes it lasted, a new personal best (or worst). When I got home, Mom would still be awake. She'd want to know what I did to ruin it and why I was so screwed up. Then something about no grandkids and away she'd go. Blah, blah, blah. Home was not an option right now.

Surprisingly the bookstore's café was packed. This apparently was the hip anti-bar scene. Bad poets, failing writers, and the intellectually arrogant, all together, happily chatting over lattés and mochas while a young guy in baggy cords played the guitar. *Why not?* I thought, peering inside. *I dig this Bohemian nonsense as much as the next guy.*

With an exorbitantly priced caramel something-or-other in one hand and my helmet in the other, I sought out a place to sit. There were no empty tables and only two with just one person. My choices were a girl in a tight, red tank top with her back toward me, or a bald dude with a Clark Gable mustache. The bald guy seemed affable enough, but the girl, based on her attractive arms and neck, somehow appeared more interesting.

With her permission I sat down. She sipped on a regular coffee and read the entertainment section of *The New York Times*. Her face, tan and round, was even prettier than her arms. A strand of long, dark hair fell onto her face. Instead of pulling it back with her hand, she blew at it, causing her to look up. That's how she caught me staring at her. I looked down, but she knew.

"Do I know you?" she asked. Her voice was sweet and girly.

I pretended to be caught off guard, like I was deep in thoughts not concerning her. "What? Oh. No, I don't think so."

She took a long look. "You seem really familiar. I used to waitress at Hall's. Have you ever eaten there?" Her left leg bounced.

"Not since I was a kid."

"Hmm," she said, now looking me up and down. "This is going to drive me nuts. Where do I know you from?"

"Do you watch much porno?" I asked. "I've been in several films."

She laughed. "Really?"

"You bet. Never actually having sex though. Just supporting roles. You know, phone company dispatcher, petting zoo attendant. Things like that." Being rewarded with more laughter, I added, "I'm surprised you recognized me without my mustache and gold chains."

"Wow, a real porno actor," she said. "I'm actually an actor, too."

"Yeah?" I said.

"Yeah. Just local theater. No porn, sadly."

"It's not a competition. I'm sure your work is of equal value."

She listed all of the plays she'd been in and the characters she'd played. She was currently in rehearsals for a production of Shakespeare's *A Midsummer Night's Dream*.

"I was actually in *A Mid-Summer Night's Cream*."

The girl winced.

"Too far?" I asked.

"A little bit." There was an awkward pause until she grinned. "I'm just giving you shit. My name's Ashley, by the way." She stuck out her arm and shook my hand.

Acknowledging my helmet, she asked, "Is that your Harley in the parking lot?"

"It's actually a Honda."

Her eyebrows raised as if she was about to speak, but no words followed. She reached into the thigh pocket of her khaki cargo pants and pulled out a pack of Marlboro Lights. "Mind if I smoke?"

Two butts already sat snubbed in a paper cup. If the store was willing to ignore their no smoking policy, I certainly was.

She placed a cigarette to her lips and patted her pockets.

"Are you looking for this?" I said, scooping a white plastic Bic from the table.

After lighting her cigarette and exhaling the first drag, she looked me over and said, "What brings you here on a Saturday night?"

"I don't know," I lied. "I just sort of ended up here. You?"

"I have play practice tonight. Don't ask me why we have it this late.

We just do. So I popped in to read the *Times*." Her eyes dropped to the newspaper, and she added, more softly, "I would sort of like to move to New York."

"To act?"

"I guess," Ashley said meekly. "I probably won't even go though, you know?" She giggled at her accidental poem.

"Why not?"

"My parents are really against it. They want me to go to college. I guess everybody thinks I'm an idiot for not wanting to go to school. It makes me feel stupid."

"Don't be ridiculous. Go to New York if you think it's the right thing."

"It's just hard to know what to do, you know?"

I took a long drink of coffee. It was getting cold and I didn't want to waste it. "You're passionate about the acting thing, right? That's all you want to do, right?"

"Exactly." Her dark eyes lit up. "But my parents think I should get my degree to have something to fall back on."

"That's always people's logic, but it doesn't make any sense. If your heart is into acting, you're not going to care about school, so you won't learn as much. Then when you do graduate, you'll jump right into your acting anyhow. After a few years your degree will be worthless because you won't remember any of it."

"That's true," she said. There was no visible change in her enthusiasm, but I could tell the argument had been filed away for the next time she discussed the point with her parents.

"Go act first. Maybe you'll make it, and you won't need anything to fall back on. But let's say after five or six years of serious commitment you haven't. Then you can go back to school."

"Good point," she said.

"You have nothing to worry about. How old are you?"

Her face squinted when she said eighteen. "How old are you?"

"Like twenty-six," I said dismissively, quickly returning to my point. "But anyway, you can go to school later if you want, and actually be interested in what you're learning. You'll only be twenty-three or twenty-four. Going to college now would just waste your parents' money."

"I totally agree," she said. "It's just hard when you disappoint your mom, you know?"

I knew a great deal about disappointing one's mother. "You've got to live your own life, though."

"I am so glad you came in here," she said, shaking my arm. "That's exactly what I think, but everyone is telling me to do the opposite."

"Listen, I did what everybody wants you to do. It's not that great. Just follow your heart. Things will work out better that way."

Ashley looked at her watch. "Damn." She reached into her backpack and pulled out her car keys. "I should probably get going." She placed the key ring around her index finger and shook the keys with her other three fingers. I smiled at her. She smiled back. No one moved.

"Is your rehearsal far away?" I asked.

"No, it's pretty close."

I stuck out my lower lip and nodded. She looked at the floor and bounced her legs. She was waiting for me to ask her out, but I just couldn't. She was only eighteen. I'm no sicko.

"I would love to go for a motorcycle ride sometime." Ashley looked away, fearing rejection.

"How about after your rehearsal tonight?"

"Awesome," she said, unable to contain her smile.

Oh crap.

Shortly after Ashley left, I retrieved a store copy of *The Four Noble Truths*, the book I bought prior to my blind date that evening. Reading would help pass the two hours until Ashley's return. The first noble truth - life is suffering. My mind drifted off. Ashley was really cute. She made these serious little faces that were absolutely adorable. *Adorable? Focus on the book. Focus on the book.*

The second noble truth - suffering is caused by desire. Three shaggy high school boys loudly entered the store, pushing each other around. They wore baggy pants and managed not to trip over their untied tennis shoes. Each of their collective six arms had at least two tattoos. The loudest boy wore his visor backwards and upside down. Their conversation was loud, ignorant, and laced with vulgarity. They annoyed me to no end. The bald man near me stopped typing on his laptop and made a face as he watched the boys.

Off his disgust I said, "I hate kids like that."

"That's how kids act nowadays," he said.

"Idiots," I replied, thinking that I better keep an eye on my bike when they left the store.

"Things have changed a lot since we were kids. I'd hate to be eighteen again," said the man.

These kids couldn't be 18. Ashley was 18. If they were the same age, then it wasn't unfathomable that one of them, or somebody just like them, dated her in the not-too-distant past.

"Oh, I don't think they're that old, are they?"

"Eighteen or nineteen, I'd guess," he said, then went back to his typing.

I wanted to go home. I didn't want to be the old guy hanging out with 18-year-olds.

But I didn't leave. I sat there, rationalizing that Ashley was a really sweet girl and that blowing her off would be rude, and she didn't deserve that. Besides she probably didn't like me anyhow. She just wanted to go for a motorcycle ride. Not wanting to hurt her feelings, I waited...and waited...and waited.

At 10:50, a young, Asian woman gently nudged me and the few others still hanging around to finish our drinks and get out. It was 50 minutes past our agreed meeting time. Ashley was a no-show. Probably for the better.

For safety's sake, I let the other cars leave the parking lot before I started my bike. Then, remembering I hadn't checked my oil in a few days, I did so. It also occurred to me that it isn't good to travel a long distance with a cold engine, so I let the bike run a few minutes before putting on my helmet. Finally, I engaged in a lengthy search of the saddlebags to retrieve my leather riding gloves, which was interrupted when a gray Jeep Wrangler pulled into the parking lot, honking. It was Ashley, puffing away at a cigarette, talking on a cell phone, and driving a stick shift, all at the same time.

As she stepped out of the Wrangler, I knew why she was late. She had changed into her "hot" clothes, a halter-top stretching tight across her chest and low-rise hiphuggers. She was built like a girl who might become a heavy woman, but that was years away. For now, everything was firm and ripe. All of a sudden I felt nervous.

"I'm so glad you're still here," she said. "I was afraid you'd be gone, and I'd never see you again."

"You just about missed me," I said, handing her a helmet.

"Do we have to wear these?"

Technically we didn't. Indiana doesn't have a helmet law. But I insisted. "My looks are my livelihood."

She laughed. "Speaking of which, what do you do?"

Maybe some honesty will scare her off. "Nothing, really. I don't work and I live with my parents."

"Really?" She looked confused.

"Yeah. I quit my job and sold all my stuff so I could find my destiny. You know, I don't want to piss my life away just going through the motions."

Ashley's big, dark eyes stared longingly for a moment. "You are the *coolest* guy I've ever met." *Ut oh, this isn't good.*

We put on our helmets and I explained the passenger rules. Never take your feet off the pegs, even when we stop, and look in the direction that we're turning. She understood and mounted the bike behind me. She put both arms around me and squeezed. *Yeah, this really isn't good.*

We went downtown on Clinton Street first. Ashley would occasionally say something, but with the noise of the engine and the helmets, I rarely understood her. I would reply with "What?" and she would just say, "Never mind."

At about the sixth stop light Ashley put her hand under my shirt and rubbed my chest hair. *Well, maybe it's sort of good.*

At the next stoplight, she leaned forward and grabbed my hands while grinding her breasts into my back. She stayed in that position for the rest of the ride. Our drive lasted a little longer than planned.

Upon our return to the bookstore, Ashley invited me to sit in her Jeep for a while and hang out.

"I better not," I said. *I had REALLY better not.*

Ashley looked hurt. "Why not?"

"I don't know. It's just sort of late and all."

"Please," she said. "Just for a little while."

Don't do it. Don't do it. Don't do it. "Okay."

"I have to warn you," Ashley said, as she unlocked her Jeep, "my car's a little messy." In fact it was filthy. Fast food bags, empty cigarette cartons, pieces of torn paper, and just general garbage littered the floorboards. You couldn't sit anywhere without getting cigarette ashes all over yourself. "I told you it was nasty."

"Oh, it's not too bad," I lied.

Ashley looked into the rear view mirror and tried to fix the mess the helmet made of her hair. "I look terrible."

"You don't look bad," I said.

"Really?" She paused. "I think you look great."

We stared at each other for a moment, then I broke. I leaned in and kissed her soft, full lips. Three little kisses, one after another.

"Thank God," Ashley said. "I'm so glad you like me." She rubbed her fingers through my hair. Placing my arms around her back I felt smooth, supple skin. I kissed her forehead. Then her nose. Then her neck. Placing her hand on my cheek, she guided me to her mouth where our tongues met. We kissed for 20 minutes.

"I should get home," I said, breathing heavily. I jumped out of the Jeep and walked over to my motorcycle. Ashley followed me and we hugged tightly. She didn't let go. Soon we were rubbing each other's backs and making out. This escalated until we were in the Jeep again, passenger seat tilted back, her on top of me, legs out the door.

I don't know how long this could have lasted, but before it could lead us any further I said, "I really better go now."

"Okay," Ashley said, now trying to catch her breath.

Ashley brought her legs into the truck straddling my stomach, "Do you want my number or anything?"

"Uh, sure," I told her. After exchanging information, we poured out of the truck a second time, only to embrace and kiss all over again.

Looking up, Ashley said, "I can't believe I'm seeing a twenty-six year old." I'd forgotten about that.

"I better get going."

If Ben Franklin was right when he opined, "Early to bed, early to rise, makes a man healthy, wealthy and wise," then I'm at serious risk of being sick, poor, and stupid. At noon the next day, I reluctantly crawled out of bed and slogged over to the computer for my "morning" ritual of checking email. I had four, two from Ashley. The morning after, I thought. The day of second thoughts and "I have a boyfriend" confessionals. Let's see what vital piece of information Ashley had forgotten to tell me last night.

Subj: Howdy
Date: July 30, 1:10 AM
From: Actingchik84
To: Vic31

Hey Bro, how ya doin'? I hope you will get this letter and you're not on the side of the road, bleeding, with a motorcycle on top of you (be careful is what I'm saying). I'm really glad I met you tonight. I haven't really clicked with anyone like that in a while. Sorry if that sounded corny. I really try to avoid sounding that dumb at all costs, but, oh well. I just got off the phone with one of my friends. I told her all about you. She thinks you sound too good to be true. I hope you're not.

I have a question for you, and I want you to be honest. Do you want to see me in my show? I know you just met me, but my show is coming up and I need to know soon what night to hold your ticket for, if you want to go. I really don't want you to go if you don't want to. I won't be mad or anything stupid like that. But if you DO go, it will make me very happy (just don't expect it to be good).

I know it's late, but this letter is making me want to talk to you, so I am going to call you right now. So if you're asleep or something when I call you can just tell me your tired and ask me to call you back...then I'll tell you to wake your ass up. So, I guess I'll just talk to you soon.

So far so good. Email #2.

Subj: Your phone sucks
Date: July 30, 2:20 AM
From: Actingchik84
To: Vic31

I don't know what's wrong with your damn cell phone, but I tried calling and it didn't work. First it rang and then it gave a busy signal. Then it rang and just stopped working. I just wanted to let you know that

```
I DID try to call you. I've got practice
tomorrow (Sun) from 2-5. But if you would
give me a call either before or after that,
it would make me very happy. So I guess good-
night and I'll (hopefully if your damn phone
works) talk to you later.
```

I replied to the first email by saying I didn't crash my motorcycle, I was really glad I met her, too, and that I did want to go to her show. Then I picked up the phone and called her.

"Hello," a woman's voice answered. It was probably Ashley's mom. This threw me for just a second. I don't like dating girls who still live with their parents, and yes, I do know that's quite hypocritical of me.

"Is Ashley there?" I asked.

"No, she's not. Do you want to leave a message?"

The answer was no, I sure didn't, but felt that I probably should. "Yeah, please tell her Vic called. She should have my number already."

"Oh," said the voice on the other end suspiciously. "I'll tell her." I sent Ashley another email to see if she wanted to meet me Tuesday evening.

I picked up *Walden* and read. I underlined a quote: *If one advances confidently in the direction of his dreams, and endeavors to live the life which he imagined, he will meet with a success unexpected in common hours.*

I found this both encouraging and troubling. "The life which he imagined." In college it was a prestigious job, a nice home and a car. I advanced confidently in that direction, and got there. But now what? I didn't know what I wanted anymore. I just knew what I didn't want. And that isn't the same thing, unfortunately.

When my parents returned home from church that day, I was lying on the couch reading. Molly was lying on the floor, begging me to rub her belly. She jumped up and ran into the kitchen to greet my parents. Mom brought in Saturday's mail, which had been neglected the day before. She tossed two envelopes on my chest and said, "Belated birthday cards." The stick-on label of the first read, *From the home of Wally and Stacy Rourke.* It had two little annoying doves kissing in a heart. I hadn't spoken to Wally since my party. The other was made out to my old lake address with a yellow forwarding sticker on the bottom right hand corner. It was from Lauren Reynolds.

"Looks like you had a good time last night," Mom said.

How could she possibly know that?

"We were already in bed before you got home from your date," she added.

My date. I had totally forgotten that I had gone out with someone else before I met Ashley. "Yeah," I said.

"That will make your aunt very happy."

"Who knows?" I took my letters upstairs to my room. Mom and Molly followed me.

Molly stood upright, front paws resting on the mattress. I reached down and lifted her onto the bed. Then I sat down beside her and rubbed my thumb between her ears.

"I want you to clean your room," Mom said.

My room was a mess. Clothes scattered all over the floor. Bed unmade, books and magazines strewn about. I'm somewhat sloppy by nature, but knowing that I would never invite a girl back to my parents' house, there was even less motivation to pick up after myself.

"What do you care?" I asked.

"I have to walk by here and it makes me angry," she said.

"I'll shut the door."

"You'll clean that room or you're not leaving this house."

Oh dear God. I needed " . . .dreams to whose direction I could advance" ASAP.

"By the way, why don't you go to church anymore?" Once she started nagging there was no stopping her.

"I don't get anything out of it."

"You do too," she said.

"All right then, what did you get out of it today?"

This stumped her. "It doesn't matter if you get something out of it. You're just supposed to go. Aren't you worried about your soul?"

"No," I said. Although, to be honest, I sort of was. "I have the same relationship with you that you have with God."

"Really," she said defiantly.

"I love you. I come to your house a lot. And I ignore everything you tell me to do."

Mom huffed at this and once again told me that I wasn't leaving the house until my room was cleaned up. Then turning to the dog she said, "Molly go pee pee." Molly barked. Mom said it again in a more excited voice, "Molly go pee pee." Molly jumped off the bed, and the pair of them went outside.

The envelope from Wally was not a birthday card, but an invitation to a couple's baby shower. Those things are supposed to be for women. Leave it to Wally to screw that up and invite men, too. And not just men, but couples for Christ sake. Did he think I'd enjoy sitting around with a bunch of married people talking about baby stuff? Fuck him. I threw the invitation away.

Lauren's was a birthday card, sort of. It was actually a *Far Side*. The one where the old west doctor is bandaging the ventriloquist's arm, while his dummy sits on a chair shot full of holes. The doctor tells him, "You'll be fine, but I can't say the same for your friend there. But from what I heard, he's the one who started the whole thing anyhow." That might appear to be a strange choice for a birthday card, but it happened to be my all-time favorite *Far Side*, so for me it was perfect.

Inside the card, written in purple ink, was this note.

Vic,

I found this card about a month ago, and remembered how it always made you laugh. Plus, I wanted to let you know I was thinking of you on your birthday. I think about you quite a bit, really. I guess after you've cared for someone you can't help but be curious as to what's going on in their life. Are you happier now? Kevin told me that you threw a huge party, then sold your house like a week later. He refuses to tell me where you live. I hope you don't think so little of me that you're worried that I'd bother you.

Anyway, I hope you're finding whatever it is you're looking for. If you ever need to talk, I'm here for you. You were one of my closest friends before and during the time we dated.

I miss you.

Lauren

To be honest, I don't remember how the card made me feel. It was definitely nice, especially, since we hadn't talked in several months. I do remember thinking that I should call her and say "hello," but I never did. As I looked for her number, Ashley called, and afterwards it was just sort of forgotten.

THE ZOO
August 3

"Did you finish *The Four Noble Truths?*" Denny said in lieu of a greeting when we met at the Fort Wayne children's zoo on Tuesday.

"Yep, it was good." We walked past the prairie dogs and into the heart of the zoo. Denny had invited me a few days after the Wizards game. He had free passes due to his "celebrity status." His words.

"Okay, let's see if you learned anything. What are the four noble truths?" Denny was springing a pop quiz on me.

"Um, well, let's see here. Life is suffering. Suffering is caused by desire. Desire can be squelched. And then the fourth one is a list of ten or twelve things to squelch it. Right livelihood. Right speech. Crap like that."

"I think maybe you should re-read the fourth truth. It's only the solution," Denny said. "But for now, let's just focus on the first one."

"Life is suffering," I said.

"Right," Denny said. "What's that mean?"

"To live is to suffer, I suppose."

"Right, but what does suffer mean?" Denny asked.

"You know, uh, have your heart broken by a girl. Not have your life work out like you hoped it would. You desire something. It doesn't happen, and you suffer."

"That's part of it," Denny said. "But I think it also deals with aging and dying. To live is to get older, which means to become frailer, and eventually die. To desire to live is to suffer."

"You think you'd be happier if you wanted to die?" I asked.

"No, because you'd still desire. It's more about not caring, just accepting."

"Yeah, but then why bother to do anything? Why not just sit under a shade tree your whole life?"

"That's for you to figure out," Denny said.

"What? Why would-"

"Aaahhtt," Denny said waving his hands at me. "No more questions."

"Yeah, but-"

"Aaahhtt," Denny said again louder. "Free your mind of questions, my young padawan learner."

I shook my head. "You're a moron."

Throughout the conversation we had never broken stride or really bothered to look closely at the animals. But with the temperature on the rise, Denny, being of generous carriage, needed to rest. On a bench in front of the seal tank, we watched jealously as the seals dove into the refreshing, cool water.

Denny pulled a piece of paper from his pocket. "I roughed out my Martin Luther King Jr. essay. Care to offer an opinion?"

"This is the thing about how it should be considered a white holiday, too?" I said, remembering our previous discussion.

"It's already a national holiday. My crux is that it should be more revered by all Americans."

I reached out to take the paper, but Denny pulled it away from me. He shook the paper a few times and cleared his throat. He then read, rather loudly. The first part was basically a reminder of what a great and brave man Martin Luther King Jr. was. He constantly received death threats, his house was bombed, and his family was endangered. He could have moved to the North and been respected, safe and wealthy. Instead, he stayed in the South and was often imprisoned.

"The only place for a just man in an unjust society is in the prisons," Denny said. "Dr. King knew his Thoreau, too. Everything's related."

"It sounds very good," I said.

"Hold on," he said, raising a finger.

"There's more?"

"Of course, there's more," he said, a little insulted. "I haven't said anything new yet."

He talked about Dr. King's opposition from within the black community. Many were full of hatred and bitterness and wanted to seek their "revenge" on the white man. Dr. King had to suffer this group's insults while trying to defuse them. Dr. King advocated speaking out against injustice through non-violence and quite likely prevented a race war.

"You certainly did your homework," I said.

"Will you stop interrupting me," he said. "I haven't said one thing that you couldn't learn by watching his biography on *A&E*."

"If it isn't important, why are you reading it to me?"

"You don't think Martin Luther King Jr. is important?" he asked, deliberately misconstruing my remark.

"What do you want from me?" I asked. "I say it's good, you say it's shit. I say it's not important, you get offended. What's the point?"

"What's the point indeed?" he said with a smile. "Now that I have your attention, I'll tell you the point."

Clearing his throat, he shook the paper and then proceeded to summarize the current state of affairs. He submitted the opinion that in the 21st century it won't be white racism but black racism which limits the black community. That in today's world it is harder for black people to transcend race because their own people refuse to let them.

"Yeah, I suppose," I said.

Denny continued. "The intelligent, talented black people feel pressure from their own race to stay 'black.' The intelligent, talented white people are free to pursue their own destinies, unconcerned with the ignorant, bitter white people. There is a victim mentality fed to the bottom holding back the middle. The top will always rise. The middle needs to say 'Enough excuses' and free themselves from the shackles of the bottom."

Denny didn't think this was only a "black" problem. The oppression blacks suffered from whites created the need for unity to begin with. America's decision to ignore racism for a hundred years after the civil war allowed Abraham Lincoln and those Union soldiers to die in vain.

"Do you have a solution?"

"Of course." He returned to his essay. "My solution is to disband all groups that defend only one race of people and replace them with groups interested in defending all human beings. With a two-part mission. First to reduce discrimination, and then to let everyone rise above the discrimination that cannot be eliminated."

Finished reading, he turned to me proudly, "Now do you get the point?"

"Yeah, I get it. You're pretending to write an essay on Martin Luther King, Jr. so you can state your opinion on black people without being called a racist."

"What the? How dare you call me a racist."

"I'm not calling you a racist," I said. "I just think you know that some people might. By speaking the praises of Martin Luther King ahead of your opinions, you're covering your ass."

Denny told me that my conclusion was, of course, absurd and that many of Thoreau and Emerson's essays were controversial in their own time, but are now regarded as brilliant.

"Have you let any of your black friends read it yet?" I asked. This was a stupid question. I should have asked if he had read it to any of his black friends yet.

"Did you not listen to the last part?" he asked, annoyed. "One of the major reasons that racism can't be eradicated is that most of the groups that fight it only represent their own race. Blacks for blacks. Jews for Jews. Hispanics for Hispanics. It doesn't-"

"I take that as a 'no'," I interrupted.

"I, as a human being, am capable of feeling for other human beings."

"You don't have any black friends, do you?"

"Do you?" he asked. Which clearly meant he didn't.

"Sort of," I said. "I worked with a black guy at Nucroix. And I'll tell you this; he wasn't suffering from shit. He made a boat load of money just because he was black."

"Do you begrudge him his income?" Denny asked.

"No, I'm just saying. In his case..."

Denny shook his head as to say "For shame, for shame," then asked if I had bothered to get to know him as a person.

"No, not really."

"Why not?" his tone dripping with judgment.

"Because he lived an hour south of me, and, you know, the opportunity never really presented itself."

Denny told me that if I had made the smallest effort with my coworker then, possibly, I would begin to understand the importance of this essay.

"Yeah, you're probably right," I said, somewhat aggressively.

Feeling refreshed from our sit, we walked into the Australian habitat. Denny was in the midst of a lecture about the difference between a wallaby and a kangaroo when I sprung the Ashley situation on him. "I met this girl I like, but she's only eighteen. Is that too young?"

"How old are you again?" He asked.

"I, uh, just turned thirty."

"So when you were her age, she was six," Denny said with a laugh.
"Yeah, that's too young."

"She's not six now," I reminded him. "She's eighteen, a legal adult."

Denny could tell that I was seeking approval, not advice. "I'm sure it's fine," he said. "As long as the age difference doesn't bother her."

I paused, debating on whether to tell him about my age lie.

"What?" he asked.

"Nothing. Let's get some drinks."

Something strange happened at the concession stand. Stepping out of line, Denny approached a married couple and said, "I'm right here, ma'am." The man's face turned red, and Denny left before they could respond.

"What was that all about?" I asked when he rejoined me.

Apparently the man kept telling the woman to "Take a look at that guy." She, with her back to Denny, kept saying, "Where? I don't see him." Throughout the rest of the day I was conscious of the stares Denny received. Children were more interested in "the fat man" than most of the animals. He may have been the most well-read, intelligent person in the zoo, but to strangers he was a freak. I chose not to say anything basically because I had no idea what to say. He knew he was fat. He knew it was unhealthy. He knew it was unattractive. He was probably more aware of those facts than anyone. Why mention it?

But still, you had to wonder. Did Denny hide himself away in his mother's house reading books and writing essays because he was too obese to engage in a healthy social life, or was it the other way around? Had his obesity freed him from all distractions?

After finishing some nachos and Cokes, we walked into the orangutan hut. Fort Wayne's two resident orangutans lived in a large glass cage with a big tree and tire swing. Both were covering themselves with newspapers like celebrities avoiding the *paparazzi*. When they peered out from the newspapers, they looked sad. It was hard to ascribe a human emotion to most other animals in the zoo but not the primates. They looked miserable.

It reminded me of a special I saw on chimpanzees. They did an experiment with adult chimps and humans two to three years old. They hid a can of Coke in a room. Then they hid a miniature Coke in a scaled-down model of the room in front of the participants. Each was led into the room. All of the chimpanzees knew immediately where the Coke was. None of the children did. Denny mentioned the gorilla they taught sign language and how it could communicate with humans.

"They're probably too advanced to be kept in zoos," I said. "They should be left in the wild and protected."

"A lot of environmentalists say that we as humans are too arrogant to accept rights of primates," Denny said. "But I don't think that's it. I think on some level, if we acknowledge that apes should be granted rights as apes and left in peace, then what about pigs, which are smart, too? What about cattle? If apes can have feelings then so can other animals. And if they have feelings, how can we in clear conscience eat them? People don't want to acknowledge the emotional aspects of any animal, because we don't want to stop eating hamburgers."

"You eat meat, right?" I asked.

"I do," Denny said shamefully. "I should stop, though. Most Eastern religions will tell you to have compassion for all of the living, breathing creatures."

I reasoned that animals eat other animals, and we have canine teeth.

Denny didn't argue the point, but did point out that we could survive without eating meat, and if we did so not for health or economic reasons, but based purely on compassion, think how much kinder we would be to each other.

Then Denny jumped. "Hot dog! I've got my next essay. I've got to get to the library and grab some Jane Goodall books."

"You don't have to go right now do you?"

"Pretty soon," he said.

We walked toward the exit.

"She thinks I'm twenty-six," I said. Denny stopped.

"That girl?" he asked. Then laughed. "You *look* twenty-six."

"What should I do?" I asked.

"Apologize to her parents." Then, interrupting me before I could protest, added, "Come on, you don't think it's a little weird that you're dating an eighteen-year-old?"

"No. I don't know. I mean I'm not proud of it or anything, but Charlie Chaplin, Woody Allen, J.D. Salinger? They all dated eighteen- or nineteen-year-olds when they were much older than me. Seinfeld did it too."

"They did great work. You have no job and live with your parents."

"So do you."

"I'm not dating teenagers."

"Famous people dating young girls is all right," I said. "But I can't?"

"When people consider you a genius, we may have to allow you certain peculiarities, but until then, it's just wrong."

ASHLEY'S FRIEND
August 3

Ashley couldn't contain her enthusiasm. She ran across the movie theater parking lot and jumped into my arms. "I'm so happy to see you again," she said, kissing my neck. With one arm still around my waist, she introduced me to her friend, Kimmy, a gangly girl with long hands and feet.

After our first meeting, the time Ashley and I had spent together was all on the phone. It was easy. We spoke for hours, exploring each other as people, what we wanted out of life, and things we had in common. The age difference was barely noticeable. Adding another eighteen-year-old to the mix changed that. We were reduced to general interest stuff, which wasn't nearly as interesting.

Apparently one of their friends was throwing a party because his parents were out of town. It was going to be huge, with a keg and everything. Kimmy asked if I wanted to come along, but Ashley quickly stepped in and thwarted it.

"There's going to be high school kids there. Vic's too old for that." Ashley laughed, I think out of pride.

"How old are you again?" Kimmy asked.

This was my moment of truth. I could just say 30, and end this little charade. When Ashley acted surprised, I could feign confusion and say it was 30 from the get-go. She would stammer awkwardly for a moment, then we'd go our separate ways. Ashley waited for my answer with that sweet, beautiful smile of hers.

"I just turned twenty-six."

"You don't look twenty-six," Kimmy said.

This comment terrified me. Did she think I looked 30? Would she want to see my driver's license?

"I told you he didn't look that old," Ashley said. I breathed again. "Dean keeps calling you 'the old man'."

"He's just jealous," Kimmy said.

I really didn't want to hear about this boy, but his name seemed to always creep into our conversations. Apparently, Dean was her best friend. They went everywhere together. It was Dean and Ashley, Ashley and Dean. I could tell early on he was going to be a huge pain in my ass.

We missed the previews because the girls needed one more cigarette before we could buy our tickets. I missed most of the movie, too. Ashley and Kimmy talked all the way through it. But since it was some mindless teen movie I really didn't care.

Arriving home much later that evening, I logged onto the Internet. Two emails, both from Ashley.

Email #11, sent during the day.

```
Subj:  You make me smile
Date: August 3, 2:14 PM
From: Actingchik84
To: Vic31
        I really liked talking to you last
night. I'm glad you called. And was surprised
you called. It made me pretty happy the rest
of the day. I really can't wait to see you
tonight. Hopefully you liked talking to me as
well. But I can never tell if a guy likes me
and likes talking to me or if they just feel
obligated to because they wanna get laid. I
hope that's not the case, but we'll see. I
really like you. But if you've decided that
you don't like me, please, tell me. Or if you
find someone else, let me know. It's just a
lot easier for me the earlier you let me
know. Ok, I'll stop saying shit like that.
I'm just paranoid...I hope. But I'm going to
stop writing now because I have just reviewed
all that I have written and I see how point-
less and unentertaining it has been. So I
will end your misery. Goodbye, and write me.
—Ashley
```

Email #12, after the movies.

```
Subj: You're hot!
Date: August 4, 1:17 AM
From: Actingchik84
To: Vic31
```

I think you're incredibly awesome and
you seem perfect for me. But we'll see what
you think. I miss you a lot right now. That
probably sounds weird but get over it. You
make me very happy. It sounds like a five-
year-old wrote this letter. I'm sure you're
in bed right now. But I am still wide awake
thinking about you. I don't know why you like
me. Maybe I never will. But I am so glad that
you do, or at least, say you do. I can't
write anymore because this letter has already
been very hard for me to write. I wish you
were here.
Ashley
p.s. Kimmy thinks you're hot!

While checking ESPN.com to see if Sammy Sosa had hit any home-
runs a mechanical voice announced, "You've got mail."

Email #13.
Subj: I'm no psycho!
Date: August 4, 2:11 AM
From: Actingchik84
To: Vic31
        By the way, I hope my letter didn't
freak you out. Hopefully, you don't think
I'm one of those psycho girls or anything,
because I definitely am NOT. It's pretty rare
that I get this anxious. My mom even noticed
it. But okay, that's starting to get stupid.
I will change the subject and disregard the
fact that a new paragraph is necessary. It is
2:15am and I'm ready to pass out. Regardless,
I'm hunched over the keyboard, like a geek. I
can't wait to move to New York. I mean I
don't want to leave you here, but I can't
wait for you to come visit me. Of course, by
that time, you'll probably be dating a new,
single mom or something and I'll be forced to
see guys that are actually my own age...shit.
I'll sign off by saying I miss you like
a bitch right now.

I quickly sent Ashley an email stating that I was awake and if she
wanted to talk on the phone to reply right now. Seconds later I received

an email.

Ashley went outside with a cordless phone so she could smoke a ciga-rette. "I hope the neighbors are asleep," she giggled. "All I have on is a T-shirt." After a pause she added, "I wish you were here right now."

Me too.

"I called Dean when I got home tonight," she said. "He's really pissing me off. All he ever does is say bad things about you."

"Like what?" I asked. He hadn't met me.

"Just like when I told him you quit your job and sold your stuff to find yourself, he said that you probably got fired, or never even had a job. That you were some pathetic liar who just said that stuff to get young girls in bed."

I started to say something to clear my good name, but she didn't let me finish.

"I know you're not a liar. Dean's just being an ass. He's so jealous of you. Like he would even know what it's like to have a real job. He's never even worked in his family's factories."

"What factories?" I asked.

"I forget what their called. Quality something or another."

"Is his last name Parrish?"

"Yeah. How'd you know that?"

"I used to know some people who worked at one of their factories," I said, and left it at that. The people were actually a person, my dad. He hated Charlie Parrish, who was probably Dean's father or uncle. According to Dad, he was a spoiled, incompetent, horse's ass who ran the business into the ground. Ralph Parrish, wo would be Dean's great grandfather, was the financial genius who created the Parrish fortune from nothing. Having made that fortune, he divorced his first wife and re-married the trophy wife who bore his children. Through selective breeding, each generation became a little better looking and a little less intelligent. Their incompetence at business caused them to lose just slightly less money than the interest from their trust funds.

"He says he wants to be an artist, but he hardly ever paints anymore. He just sits around and bitches all the time. He's so negative."

"Why don't you just stop hanging out with him then?"

She started talking about what good friends they were in high school again, but I interrupted. "You know what Ashley? I really don't care about Dean. I want to talk about you."

RUBBER MALLET
August 9

"It's about time you dragged your ass in here," I yelled at Kevin, when he finally strolled into the Rubber Mallet. This rotting, old country bar was Kevin's little hideaway from the world. Whenever things slowed down in his sales territory he would give me a call and we'd meet up at noon. Or at least, I would. Kevin was generally late.

The waitress, seated at the end of the bar yelled, "You boys want cheeseburger platters?" She only got up when the job required it, and just taking an order didn't.

"Yep," Kevin yelled back.

"You hear that, Pat?" she said to one of the men sitting next to her watching the Cubs on television. He had, and said he'd take care of it at soon as the inning was over.

"And put them on one tab," I added.

"You buying?" Kevin asked.

"No, you are." I looked at my watch. It was 12:35. "For making me wait."

"Gee, I hope I didn't throw off your day planner." He loved giving me little digs about not working. "I'll tell you what. Loser pays." We traditionally played pool to decide who'd buy lunch. I'm horrible at pool, so I almost never won. But it really didn't matter because Kevin (or Nucroix) bought anyway. He just wanted to gamble.

"Let me ask you something," I said to Kevin as he racked. "You ever been to a couple's baby shower?"

"No. Kylie goes to all that crap. Occasionally, I get together with another husband and play golf or something."

It was my break. I smacked the cue ball with all of my might and barely altered anything.

"Weak," Kevin chuckled. With force, he hit the cue ball back into the crowd, scattering them all over the table. A solid fell in. He took aim at another and missed. "I've never even heard of a couples baby shower," he added. "Who's having one?"

"Numb nuts Wally." I lined up a shot.

"He's dragging the men into it?"

"Yep," I said, missing horribly.

After knocking in three more solids, Kevin asked if I was going.

"Nope."

"Sending a gift?"

"Nope." Concentrating on a stripe that was inches from the corner pocket, I pulled back the cue and fired, knocking it in, but scratching as well.

Kevin retrieved the cue ball. "Isn't Wally one of your best friends?"

"He was, I guess."

"Then you should send him a gift." Kevin knocked in another solid.

"That's just it," I said, as he continued to play. "Why do I have to buy him something every time his life changes? He gets married. I buy a gift. And I was in the wedding, so I had to rent a tuxedo, too. I think if you get married you should tell people that if they pay for a dress or tuxedo, they shouldn't have to buy anything else."

"That's not how it works, though." Kevin lined up his shot. "You just make sure you get it all back at your own wedding."

"I may never get married. I may never have a baby. So what about me?"

Kevin laughed. "Then you're going to save so much money, you won't need any gifts."

The platters arrived. With the exception of a few fries, they would be ignored until our game ended. The only solid left was the eight ball. Kevin had a relatively tough shot because all of the stripes blocking the pockets. He finally decided on a bank shot, which went in, but so did the cue ball.

"Damn it," he yelled.

"Kicked your ass again," I told him.

"Oh, hey, I almost forgot," Kevin said, when we finally sat down to eat. "Lauren Reynolds has another boyfriend."

"She does, huh?" I found that information strange, based on her card, but for the most part, didn't care.

"Yeah," he laughed. "And get this, he's a bigger bum than you. He's like thirty-five, tends bar part time, and that's it. He's moved in with

Lauren, so basically, she's supporting him."

That did capture my attention. "Is he really good-looking or something?"

"No, he's just average-looking, I guess. Tall and skinny with dark hair. Basically, she just went out and found another you."

"Is he all cool-acting then?"

Kevin missed the joke. "I haven't met him, but he went with her to a company reception, and I heard he was a real jackass."

"That doesn't make any sense to me," I said.

"It does to me. You rattled her confidence. She's probably never been dumped before, and then you stepped in and did it. And for no reason, just because you wanted to be a bum."

"Would you stop calling me a bum?" I interrupted.

"Okay. What are you then?" he asked.

I thought of Denny. "I'm a transcendentalist."

"I don't understand half the shit you talk about anymore, but you're a fool if you don't try to get back with her."

"Now you just told me she's living with a guy. What chance would I possibly have?"

"Every chance. Don't you see? You're the guy who got away. The puzzle she couldn't solve. That's why she's dating this bum."

"Hey!"

"What? I'm talking about him. Is he a *transdentist* too?" Kevin said. "I'm just saying you could get back in there."

"Man, you need to give up your little fantasy about me and Lauren."

"Good point. Why would you want to be with a beautiful woman who would support you, when you can live with your parents?"

"Here's why we'll never get back together," I said, waving a French fry. "I'd be right back where I started. It would make this whole thing pointless." Kevin raised his finger to dispute my reasoning, but I refused to give up the floor. "Besides, I'll have you know, I'm seeing someone new."

This piqued his interest. I gave him a fairly accurate description of Ashley and how we met.

"This girl sounds pretty good. What does she do for a job?"

"She doesn't really have one."

Kevin threw his hands in the air. "That seems to be the trendy thing these days. How does she get money?"

"I don't know for sure. I never asked."

"She has to have money. How does she pay her bills?"

"I don't think she has many," I said.

"Rent?"

"Lives with her parents."

"She can't make fun of you then. Car payment?"

"Parents," I said.

"God damn. Is she spoiled or something?"

"Doesn't seem too bad."

"Really. I would keep an eye on her about that. She still has her parents paying all of her bills. No job. That doesn't bode well. How old is she?"

I didn't answer right away, because my mouth was full and it's rude to talk in that condition. I swallowed. Kevin asked about her age again. I took a drink of Coke.

"She's not in college?" he asked.

"No," I said.

"Thank God. You scared me for a second. Like twenty-two or three?"

"Closer to twenty," I said.

He wanted to know how much closer. I told him 18. He sat frozen for a minute. Finally, he said, "Eighteen, huh?"

"Yep," I said. "But she's an old soul."

"You were probably fourteen when she was getting potty-trained."

"Maybe, but that's all behind us now."

Kevin wanted to know what her parents thought. What my parents thought. If I bought her alcohol. If I was going to the prom. Would I be wearing her class ring on a chain around my neck? And what he considered his *pièce de résistance*, did I have to notify my neighbors that I was a pedophile? After he did what he considered a hilarious ten minutes on the subject, I told him the rest of the details. Including the part about her thinking I was 26.

"You only want what you can't have," Kevin said, now being serious. He'd made this argument several times in the past. "You know dating an eighteen-year-old won't work out, and you like it. You don't have to commit."

"Not this shit again, please."

"You have to at least consider it," Kevin demanded. "It affects your whole life. You say you quit your job because you wanted to search for something. But maybe you don't. Maybe you're pissing away your life and you don't even understand why. Think about it."

"You boys want pie?" the waitress yelled from her barstool.

Kevin declined, but I ordered a slice of pecan, warmed. "God damn it," Kevin said. "I can't just sit here and watch you eat that. Two pieces."

"So what do you think I should do?" I asked.

"Get yourself out of it before it becomes a huge mess."

"No, I mean do you think I should tell her I'm thirty?"

"You might as well. Does it matter really? It's just four years. If she likes older men, it will probably excite her. But I'm telling you, for your own sake, get out of this." After a pause, he added, "I guarantee you she can't be significantly better looking than Lauren."

"It's not that," I said.

"Then what is it?" he asked. "The conversation?"

"I don't know. It's just that she, I don't know, makes me like who I am, I guess."

He laughed in my face. "What's that, the cradle-robber part or the liar part?"

"Man, you suck."

THE MOTHER
August 19

My dashboard clock read 4:03 p.m. I had been driving around Ashley's housing development for the last half an hour. We had agreed to meet at 4:00 and I saw no reason to get there a moment early.

Three weeks into our relationship, Ashley wanted me to meet her parents. I was dreading it. Ordinarily, I'm at ease in the living room, but in this case I feared they'd ask my age or when I graduated from high school. I didn't know which would be more uncomfortable, telling the truth or lying. I wanted to get out of it, but it seemed so important to Ashley that I was unable to refuse.

Actually, the thought of being found out was so horrifying that I did refuse, but Ashley cut a deal with me. The weekend of her play, my parents were going on a three-day trail ride with some of their horse friends. If I agreed to meet her parents Friday before the show, she would spend the next two nights alone with me. She might've anyhow, but it was a carrot I wasn't willing to risk.

Out of the several housing developments on Old Auburn Road, Ashley's parents lived in the nicest. They owned a two-story yellow house overlooking a golf course. I parked on the cul-de-sac behind Ashley's Jeep and entered through an open garage door. Two of the parking spots were empty, and the third stored a covered sports car. This was encouraging. Maybe Ashley's parents weren't home. I rang the doorbell and the garage door began to close. Whoops. Not a doorbell. I quickly hit it again, then knocked.

Ashley opened the door and swung her arms around my neck. She had on a long, pink Koala bear T-shirt. Her thick, tangled hair hinted that her pillow might still be warm. "Hi, Sweetheart," she said grabbing my hand. She led us into the living room and sat me down on a leather couch. She sat on my lap and played with my hair.

Looking down the hall, I asked, "Is anybody home?"

"Mom's in the next room, but she doesn't care." She tried to kiss me.

Ashley laughed when I tensed up. "I'm just kidding. Mom's getting groceries and Dad's at work."

"You should be getting ready then, so we can leave."

"We can't leave until my dad gets here. I promised him he could meet you." She gave me a little kiss. "We might as well enjoy ourselves."

"Yeah, but if you got ready now, we could leave, like, right away or something."

"Will you stop?" she said. She turned on my lap to face me, naked knees straddling my waist. She ran her hands through my hair and rocked back and forth, grinding on me.

I decided at that moment to tell her I was 30. Right then and there, but a car pulled into the driveway before I could. Ashley jumped off my lap. "The rest will have to wait until tonight." She ran toward the hallway.

"Where are you going?" I asked.

"To get ready." She disappeared around the corner, leaving me alone on the couch.

The door opened and Ashley's mom carried in two bags of groceries. She was a skinny woman with red hair and bright red lipstick.

"Ashley," she yelled. Not waiting for a response, she continued, "I almost ran the Land Rover into the garage door. It's either all the way up or all the way down."

"What?" Ashley yelled from another room.

I walked into the kitchen. "Hello. I'm Vic. I'm here to pick up Ashley."

"Oh, okay," she said. Her eyebrows had been plucked out and replaced with some sort of penciling. It took effort not to stare.

"I was the one who lowered the garage door. I thought it was a doorbell. Sorry."

She made an "I can see how that might happen" face.

"Would you like me to help you bring in the groceries?"

"No, that's okay." She returned to the garage.

Alone in the living room, I looked at the pictures of Ashley and her two brothers on the piano. The oldest brother looked a lot like Ashley, with wavy hair and dark eyes. He was pictured with his wife and baby. The middle brother had red hair and freckles like their mom. He was still in college. The playbill from Ashley's show sat on the piano bench. I carried it into the kitchen and waved it at Ashley's mom. "Did you see it already?"

"Uh-huh," she said, filling the refrigerator. "We went last night."

"Was it good?"

"It was a little rough to be honest with you. But hopefully they'll have all the bugs worked out tonight." Then she added, "Ashley's good in it, though."

"She sure loves acting," I said.

"She sure does," her mother replied sourly, like it had become a problem. For the first time since I'd entered the kitchen, she stopped unpacking. "What do you think about her moving to New York?" Her voice softened. She hoped we'd become allies in keeping her baby in Indiana.

"I think she should go. If she loves it, then it will be the right thing. If she hates it, she can move on with the rest of her life."

She turned cold. "I think her not going to college would be a huge mistake." After a few moments of silence I crept back into the living room. Ashley crossed the hall wrapped in a towel. She gave me a quick wave as she entered her room. Sticking her head out the door, she yelled, "Mom, who's all coming tonight?"

Her mom yelled from the kitchen, "Your grandma, your Aunt April, your Aunt Kate, and some of your cousins." *Great. More potential questions.*

"When are they getting here?" Ashley asked.

"At six," her mom replied.

"We'll be gone by then," Ashley yelled.

Her mom came marching into the living room. "No, you will not. They're coming to support you in your play. You're going to be here to greet them."

Ashley slammed her door. From the living room you could hear it lock. Her mom looked at me, "Oh, that girl."

Smiling, I shrugged like an idiot.

Half an hour later Ashley appeared dressed and ready to go. Her mom immediately jumped her. "Ashley, change out of my shirt." Ashley had on a black tank top.

"I'm borrowing it."

"No. You don't take care of things."

"Yes, I do."

"Oh really?" her mom challenged. "What about the pit stains you left in my white one?"

Ashley looked at me horrified. "That was not me."

Seeing the humiliation she had caused her daughter, she backed off a little. "Either way, I want you to change."

"No," Ashley said, petulantly. "I'm wearing it!"

"No, you're not!"

"Yes, I am!"

"Then you're at least going to stay here long enough to say hello to your grandma."

"Stop telling me what to do!" Ashley yelled.

"Maybe I would if you'd grow up!"

The next five minutes was a blur of screaming accusations and counter-charges, building to a "Go fuck yourself!" from Ashley.

"Why, is that what you do?" her mother shot back, too angry to realize what she was saying (I hope).

"No," Ashley screamed. "I can still get somebody else to do it for me." Then without missing a beat, added, "Come on Vic, we're leaving." I had never been more uncomfortable in my entire life.

Ashley's mom glared at me. Once again I smiled and shrugged at her.

"Come on Vic," Ashley repeated.

"It was nice meeting you," I said. There was no response.

PANIC ATTACK
August 19

Ashley was incredible in her part. It was obvious she had a gift. She was so much better than most of the other actors that the play seemed uneven. How could her mother watch this performance and not want her to pursue her dream?

Her mother's trepidation was not shared with the rest of the family though. After the show, Ashley was surrounded by aunts and cousins telling her how great she was. "We just know you're going to be famous some day." Her mom stood off to the side sulking, but her dad beamed. I had sat beside him at the show and he laughed the hardest at the jokes and clapped the loudest in the end. After one of Ashley's scenes, I whispered to him, "She's pretty great, isn't she?"

"I certainly think so." His smile highlighted how much Ashley resembled him.

I was invited to join everyone at the Pizza Hut, but declined, telling some lie about leaving town for the weekend. Ashley went with them and was picked up there by her friend Kimmy, under the pretense of spending the night. Shortly thereafter, Ashley was transferred to me at the bookstore parking lot, so we could begin our romantic tryst.

"I told you the play sucked," Ashley said as we drove up Interstate 69.

"You were unbelievable. I was proud of you."

"Oh! Thank you." Ashley kissed me on the cheek. "I could tell my dad really liked you."

"That's nice. I liked him, too."

"Even before they met you, my mom was complaining that you were too old for me, but my dad was like, 'If he makes her happy, what's it matter?' Isn't that cool?"

I couldn't take it anymore. I felt guilty. I felt ashamed. But mostly I felt stupid. I had to tell her the truth before things went any further.

"Ashley," I said. "I need to tell you something."

Her face flashed terror. "Oh God, you're married."

"No," I laughed.

"You don't want to go out with me anymore?" Before I could answer she was reeling off excuses about the play. "I knew I shouldn't have let you come to the play. The director screwed the whole thing up." She felt that me liking her or disliking her was related to her performance in a play. If there's any group more neurotic than performers, I haven't met them.

"Will you stop?" Her reaction actually made me happy. The things in her imagination were so much worse than the truth that this should be easy. I would just tell her my age, and she would say, "Is that all?" And we would both be relieved.

"Ashley, I'm not twenty-six."

She tilted her head in confusion. "How old are you?"

"I just turned thirty."

I believe the clinical term is panic attack. Her whole body shook. "I can't breathe. I can't breathe," she gasped. After struggling to roll down the window she burst into uncontrollable sobs. Long, hard gasps for air intermixed with bawling.

I was completely unprepared for this reaction. "I'm so sorry. I'll take you home right now, and we'll forget this whole thing happened."

Ashley's reply was more bawling.

"Just don't freak out," I said, but that ship had sailed. "Next exit, I'll turn around and take you home."

I sped up for a second to get to an exit quicker, but then regained my senses and slowed back down to the legal speed of 65 mph. I couldn't risk getting pulled over by a state policeman in Ashley's current condition. I wasn't doing anything illegal, but the thought of having to answer the question as to why she was crying was enough to make me drop the speed to 63, just to be safe.

Finally, Ashley was able to speak. "I don't want to go home. Let's just go to your house. But don't talk to me for a minute. I have to think." Ashley tried to light a cigarette but couldn't. Her hands were shaking too furiously. I snatched her lighter, and lifted it to the cigarette in Ashley's lips and she greeted the flame with a deep inhale and a haze of smoke filled my car.

We drove to my house in silence, with the notable exception of her occasional fits of bawling. Ashley stared out her window, unable to look at me. When we finally got home Ashley wanted some privacy to call Kimmy. Her cell phone couldn't find a signal so she used the telephone in my bedroom as I waited elsewhere.

What had so drastically changed? I was the exact same person. I hadn't lied about anything other than my age. But I tried to put myself in Ashley's position. When I was 18, 30 seemed ancient. She probably had teachers younger than me. If she were a freshman in college, dating a senior would have been a big deal, and he would have been eight or nine years my junior.

After 45 minutes, Ashley stepped out of my room smoking a cigarette. She hadn't stopped chain smoking since I told her.

"All right," she said very seriously. "I'm not going to dump you. But we're going to take things, much, much slower."

"That's good," I said. But I didn't mean it. I'd always felt uncomfortable, but now it was completely strange.

Lying on my bed beside me, Ashley said, "I'm glad you told me. I still love you, I just need some time to get used to this."

We hugged. I tried to kiss her, but Ashley was having no part of that. We were on my bed, fully clothed, as Ashley smoked a cigarette in silence. Silence through most of the next cigarette as well, until finally Ashley said, "If you were twenty-six we'd be having sex right now." Which of course is ageism, but I opted not to sue. Neither of us slept that night, but both of us pretended we were. At 7:00 a.m. I drove her home.

Ten minutes after dropping Ashley off, my cell phone rang. There was crying on the other end. "Vic, I'm so sorry. But I think we should break up. I don't want to. It's just, the age difference is too much."

I didn't argue.

THE PUSH
August 20

At noon, Mom returned home with the horse trailer. Two things were strange about this. She was a day early, and she was alone. After putting the horses in the barn she marched straight to my room. Fortunately, my door was locked, keeping her from barging in and seeing me in my pathetic state.

"Wake up," Mom yelled. "You're dad's been bit in the nuts by a tick. You have to mow the yard." Molly, at Mom's feet, chimed in with a bark.

"What?"

Molly barked again.

"Not you."

"Open up this door!" Mom was in one of her frantic moods where everything has to happen immediately.

All morning I'd been lying in the fetal position, thinking about Ashley, and weathering waves of emotion. The last person I wanted to deal with at this moment was my mother.

She banged on the door. "Wake up. You've slept long enough." I hadn't slept at all. "Your dad's in the hospital."

"What happened?" I asked.

"He got bit in the nuts by a tick. His bag's all swollen up."

Now this was the second time I heard her say that, and my mind still couldn't seem to process the information. "When?"

"Yesterday and today. Now go mow the yard."

Maybe I'm dense, but first of all, I failed to see the correlation between engorged gonads and lawn maintenance. Secondly, if my father was in the hospital, that seemed the higher priority. "Shouldn't I go see Dad, first?"

"No. He'll be back in an hour. I just wanted to bring the horses back."

"I don't, uh, what are they doing to him?" I still lacked cohesion.

"Just a shot. He can't work for a week, though. He has to go to the doctor's every day and get a shot in the rear. Then he'll come home and watch TV. He'll love it."

There was a Wizards game in just under two hours. I hoped to meet Denny there to take my mind off Ashley. "Can I do it tomorrow?"

"No. Because of your dad we had to come home." She said this like Dad was whining about the weather or something trivial. Apparently she couldn't fathom how a swollen scrotum might make horseback riding less pleasurable. "Now all of our horse friends are coming over tonight, and the yard needs to be mowed." I was about to agree when she delivered the final blow, in her cocky voice. "I'm sick of you never lifting a finger around here. You are mowing that yard before you leave, and that's that." I hate that cocky voice.

If Mom could've seen me, she would have known that I was upset, so I stalled. "Does the rider have enough gas?"

"Nobody's allowed to use the rider except your dad," she yelled through the door. "He thinks we'll screw it up."

My parent's yard is just shy of two acres. The baseball game was in an hour and a half. "No way," I said. "I'm not mowing the entire yard with the push."

"Yes you are." Again, with the cocky voice. "Now get out here."

"I'll do it." I said, not wanting to waste any more time arguing. "But in a little bit. You go on back to the hospital."

"You better have it done before I get back," she yelled.

"I will."

I heard her snort. "You better. And don't you use that rider."

I yelled, "I won't." But the second she was gone I went outside and used it anyway.

If my parents had returned just five minutes later they would have never been the wiser. But with only two laps to go in the front yard they pulled into the driveway. I only took my eyes off the yard for a split second to wave. That was long enough. Something jarred the mower so hard it nearly threw me off the seat. I clung to the steering wheel with both hands, causing the mower to make a hard right.

The noise was deafening. "WaWaWaWaWaWa." Loud and penetrating, "WaWaWaWaWaWa." Whatever I hit had pushed part of the mower deck into the blades. This friction would have stripped several gears had the tractor not circled back into a tree. The head on collision killed the engine, saving the deck. Dad, who hadn't been home more than 20 seconds, gingerly climbed out of the truck. With swollen balls, a sore ass, and a disgusted look on his face, he slowly walked to meet me.

"I told your mom I didn't want you on the God damn thing," he said. I finished up with the push mower.

THE IDIOT FAN
August 20

"The Wizards couldn't beat a good high school team," I heard a man yell when I arrived at the Castle in the second inning. The Peoria pitcher had just struck out a Wizard's player to finish off the side and some jackass was taunting the home crowd. "Hell," the man continued, "your guys couldn't even beat a *bad* high school team."

When I made it to my seat, Denny was staring blankly at the field, his arms crossed, resting on his belly. His jaw muscles flexed, and he barely even said hello.

Some sports fans mistake supporting a team for being on the team. What's worse, those people often perceive you as a member of the opposite team and start competing. We were dealing with such a fan this day, and his irritating behavior bordered on intolerable.

As the Wizards took the field he yelled, "Somebody better tell your pitcher that this isn't softball."

"That's not even clever," I said, turning back to see the guy. "How long has this been going on?"

"Since the first pitch," Denny said, disgusted. "This guy's not good enough to play, yet he's abrasive because the team he chooses to like is beating the team we choose to like."

"Best to ignore him, I guess. Don't give him the satisfaction of a retort." I couldn't have cared less about the guy, or even the game for that matter. On the motorcycle ride up, I thought about traveling. Between the Ashley debacle and my parents' mounting scorn, a pilgrimage seemed to be an attractive alternative to a melt down at home.

"You ever feel like getting away and going somewhere?" I asked.

Denny thought this question was in reference to the taunting behind us. "I would prefer he did."

"No, I mean in general. You know, take a trip somewhere."

"No. Not really. Why would I?"

"To broaden your experiences," I said. "Just get out and go some-

where. You want to be a writer? Go to Paris like Hemingway and
Fitzgerald."

"Just when I think that you're making progress, you start spewing out
this moronic, unimaginative crap," Denny said. I tried to interrupt, but
this clearly was going to be a long rant. "Aspiring writers who are fans of
the lost generation want to go to Paris. The Beat generation idiots want
to go to Manhattan or start hitchhiking. I'm a Thoreau guy. Do I live in
the woods? No. You know why?"

"You might get bit in the nuts by a tick."

"Because it's been done, that's why," Denny said, continuing his dis-
sertation. "It doesn't matter how many letters of introduction you have,
you can't meet Gertrude Stein. Kerouac is dead, too. And if he were
alive, we probably wouldn't like each other. It's not about the location.
It's about the community. It's about future icons still young, hungry and
unsure of their own genius encouraging each other. *That* can happen anywhere. So I think I'll stay right here in Fort Wayne and write about the
downtown Coney Island hotdog stand."

I was a bit skeptical about the prevalence of young, hungry geniuses
in the greater Fort Wayne area but chose to continue my rebuttal along
its original lines. "How are you going to know what it means to be here
unless you see someplace else for a change? You'll never know what's
special or shitty about this place until you see some other stuff."

Denny was about to retort, when the Peoria first baseman hit a home
run. The hill-Jack behind us started up again. "He's throwing softballs,"
he said, and then slid into other equally insightful remarks such as, "the
Wizards suck." Denny's ears turned red with anger. People in the stands
were reaching their breaking points. "Hey, why don't you just shut up?" a
large woman in a NASCAR T-shirt yelled. Someone else threw a plastic
beer cup. The displays of hatred only seemed to fuel his behavior. He
yelled "Whew," over and over for no particular reason. A man with two
young children shouted, "Get your ignorant ass out of here!" The obnoxious fan, a wiry little rat whose hair cut just bordered on a mullet, was
undeterred. "I paid for my ticket the same as you. I ain't going nowhere."

It was at this point I smelled one of the most disagreeing odors my
nose has ever been so unfortunate to inhale. There seemed but one possible source – Denny. In a few innings, these nasty barbs would likely be
aimed at Denny's dancing, and apparently it was making him nervous. I

felt for him, no one enjoys being publicly ridiculed, but I couldn't endure the flatulence long enough to be of much comfort.

"Hey, I'm going to get a drink," I said, trying not to breathe out of my nose.

Over the next few innings, I hung around the concession stand and pined for Ashley. To cheer myself up, I listed all the reasons why I was better off without her. She was spoiled and melodramatic, and trying to have discussions with her friends was torture. It backfired. I felt worse, because I knew it was a lie. As much as I shouldn't, as stupid as it was, I really did like her. Instant nausea. Overwhelming nausea. I rushed into the men's room and vomited into a urinal.

After cleaning myself up, I rejoined Denny, who was midway through his pre-dance stretching. "Look at this," he said nervously, pointing at the stands. Usually by the seventh inning the seats behind the Wizards dugout were filled to capacity. Today, half the people had cleared out. "That idiot ran them all off," Denny said. Sure enough "that idiot" and his friends sat alone in Denny's prime cheering section.

From the overhead speakers the announcer yelled, "Ladies and gentlemen, who feels like dancing?" Denny made the lonely climb to the top of the dugout as I stood point. If that jackass fan yelled one disparaging remark, I would punch him in the mouth. I ordinarily loathe violence, mostly because I'm a coward, but on this particular day, a fight might be a welcome substitute for what I currently felt.

The song *du jour* was, "Now That We Found Love," by Heavy D. The fear of being mocked caused Denny's dancing to be hesitant. The fan stood up. I prepared to attack. But he said nothing. He and his friends walked down the steps, passed Denny without incident, and disappeared into the bathroom.

With the threat of his heckling removed, Denny ratcheted the dancing to full speed. His flabby arms fluttered above his head, in time with his thrusting pelvis. The crowd bathed him in cheers.

The song finished. Denny accepted his standing ovation, then rejoined me at his seat. The game resumed, and the obnoxious fan returned to continue his belligerence.

"I thought for sure that dickhead would yell something when you were dancing," I said.

"Nah," Denny said, calmly wiping himself down with a towel. "I knew he wouldn't. This is *my* house."

BACK IN LOVE

Arriving home that evening, I quickly sidestepped my parents and their friends, and went to my room. I was hoping that Ashley may have emailed me, and to my relief, she had.

Post break-up email #1.

```
Subj:  I still love you
Date: August 20, 3:43 PM
From: Actingchik84
To: Vic31
         I can't handle this. I feel like shit.
Thank God, I have a show tonight to take my
mind off it for a little bit. I keep crying
like a baby. Kimmy says that the right deci-
sions are the ones that hurt the most. But
how can I be sure I'm right? I know I have no
room to say this right now, but the thought
of you just touching or kissing another girl,
infuriates me. I honestly do love you. I just
need to make sure you know that. Maybe all I
need is some time. God, that sounds so
cliché. I understand if you don't want to
wait around, though. I just want to say again
that I will not be seeing anyone else. I
promise. I still really want you to come see
me in New York next month. Very badly. But I
completely understand if you either feel that
there's no point or you no longer have any
interest in doing that. That's fine. I know
how much I miss you now and it'll only get
worse. You are a wonderful and incredible
person. And I WANT to be with you, but I'm
not totally convinced that that is the right
decision. Anyway, I'm very sorry to write
this shit to you. I'm sure you think its
bullshit. I know I'm a bitch. But I love you
and I'm so very, very sorry.
Ashley
```

I'd always been conscious of it, but at this point I was extra careful about not writing anything too incriminating over email, since a permanent record could be saved. What could be done with that record I had no idea, but for some reason, it concerned me.

My reply:

```
RE: I still love you
Date: August 20, 8:59 PM
From: Vic31
To: Actingchik84
        It's probably good we broke up. I do
care about you, but the age difference made
me feel really uncomfortable sometimes. I
think after we've both had time to think
about it, if we still want to be together
maybe we could try again. If not, I will
always be your friend if you want me to be.
```

Then I went to bed, exhausted. The next morning I received two emails. A short one to warn me she was calling, then this.

Post break-up email #3.

```
Subj: I'm so confused?
Date: August 21, 2:47 AM
From: Actingchik84
To: Vic31
        Okay. So I was a big pussy and didn't
call you. Sorry. It's 3 a.m. anyway so I just
figured you'd think I was psycho. Listen,
about how long do you think I should wait
this shit out? Because I know right now that
I miss you very much. And I obviously regret
it. But how long do you think I should wait?
It kind of bothers me that you feel we needed
to break up, too. Because you seemed to think
it was perfectly all right. I really really
hate this unsure feeling I have. But I know
if I do decide to get back together with you,
I want to be 100% sure. Because I don't want
to ever have to go through this again. It
makes me sick and depressed. But I'll shut up
about all that and we can talk tomorrow.
```

That afternoon Ashley called and we talked for two hours. Mostly about how much we missed each other, and how we were holding up. I couldn't eat. Ashley couldn't stop. In the end, Ashley said, "I love you so much, that this is killing me."

"I love you, too," I said. Ashley broke into uncontrollable sobbing. I waited until she composed herself, then we hung up. My appetite returned.

Waking up the next morning, I immediately turned on my computer.

Post break-up email #4.

```
Subj: Howdy
Date: August 22, 1:39 AM
From: Actingchik84
To: Vic31
        I'm going to try and keep this short
and sweet because it's nearly 2 a.m. and I
have to wake up at 8:30 a.m. I'm glad I
talked to you today. One thing I've noticed
about this relationship is now that we've
"broken up" I have nothing bad to say about
you. I was talking to Dean and I know he
wanted me to talk negative about you but I
just couldn't. I kept saying how sad I was
because I love you and if you weren't you're
age, nothing would've changed. There was no
personality flaw or anything. Just your damn
age. I think you're completely wonderful. I
wouldn't change a thing about you.
```

"You've got mail."

Post break-up email #5.

```
Subj: I WANT YOU BACK!!!!
Date: August 22, 12:11 PM
From: Actingchik84
To: Vic31
        You know what, I'm being a dumb bitch.
Let's get back together. I hope you haven't
changed your mind and don't want to. If you
don't I understand, but I really, really hope
that you do want to. I couldn't stand to
hear it if you didn't. So if you don't want
to, email me. If you do want to, call me.
But do it quick. I move to New York in a
week.
```

I picked up the phone.

Being with Ashley her last week in Fort Wayne was wonderful. Every day we went for long motorcycle rides in the country, pulling over when we happened across "pretty places to talk." Ashley broached the subject of sex just once, asking if we could wait for New York, to make it more special. I didn't mind. I appreciated every moment we shared that week.

"My mom is still fighting me about New York. She doesn't want me to go. She basically tells me that I'm a selfish, naive, little girl."

"Your mom's probably just worried about you."

"I know," she replied. "But I don't know how to make it any better. I told her that I wouldn't do anything stupid. But she said that I have no idea what the world is like. Of course, I don't. How am I supposed to know if I don't go and find out? You have to start somewhere. I can't help it if I'm young, or that I never lived in New York before."

"Once you're there and get adjusted, she'll be fine."

"Maybe." Ashley kissed my hand. "I don't want to bore you anymore with this shit."

"It's not boring."

"I know it is. But you're the only person who isn't negative about it. Kimmy doesn't want me to go because she'll miss me. My parents don't want me to go. Even Dean is being all negative. He's like, 'You know there's already a million actors there.' I know that. I know I won't be shit there. But you have to go and try, don't you? I swear to God, I don't know why he's moving there with me."

I'm pretty sure I did. "Is he going to be a pain in the ass when I come out to see you?" I asked. I was waiting three weeks for Ashley to get settled before my visit.

"Who cares if he is?" she said.

"How big is this guy?" I asked.

"He's pretty small."

"In that case," I laughed, "who cares if he is?"

NEW YORK
September 1

Ashley's first week in New York made her homesick. We talked on the phone for several hours every night. She would discuss her day, her apartment situation and Dean. She would complain about Dean being selfish, or Dean being lazy, or Dean being blah, blah, blah. I mostly blocked it out. Each night before we said good-bye, Ashley would tell me how much she missed me, and how wonderful "our special event" would be when I arrived. After hanging up, we'd email each other.

New York email #5.

```
Subj: I Love You more and more each day!
Date:  September 1, 11:31 PM
From: Actingchik84
To: Vic31
          I told you on the phone all the crap
     that happened to me today.  But I still want to
     write you, just so I can feel close to you or
     whatever. I guess what I'm trying to say is
     that I miss you.  So hurry up and get your
     ass out here.
     Love forever and ever to eternity,
     Ashley
     PS I love you more.
```

As I replied, Mom barged into my room. "You're not seeing that girl from your Aunt Barb's church."

"I know that," I said, closing my email.

"Nice of you to tell me. I would still think you were if I hadn't said something to Barb. I said, 'It sure looks like that blind date worked out.' That's when she told me the humiliating truth."

"Humiliating?" I said. "That's a little strong."

"That girl keeps bringing you up in the 'prayers and concerns!' Every week. And she refers to you as Jack and Barb's nephew who joined a cult."

"What cult?" I asked.

"The Buddhism cult."

"I've read two books!"

"You're supposed to be a Catholic," she yelled back.

"Why do I have to *be* anything? Everybody thinks they have to belong to something, which means something else has to be wrong. I'm sick of it. Black vs. Whites. Jews vs. Muslims. Republicans vs. Democrats. Gays vs. Straights. I'm through with teams. I'm not anything. I'm just me."

"Your father was right. You are gay."

"I'm not gay."

"You just said you were."

"You missed the point. I was - Dad thinks I'm gay?"

"You aren't dating anyone."

"Actually, I am. I met her the same night I had the blind date. That's who I've been seeing."

"Is it serious?" she asked.

"I don't know. I really like her. More than anyone I've liked in a long time."

Mom softened. "Would you like to invite her over for dinner?"

"I can't. She just moved to New York City."

"New York City! Why do you even bother to get my hopes up?"

"So you won't think I'm gay," I said. "Besides I'm going to go visit her in a week. You never know."

"How long are you going for?" Mom asked.

"Until she tells me to leave, I guess."

Mom exhaled through her nose as she quickly turned her head. "Make sure your room is clean before you go."

Mentioning Ashley to my mother seemed to jinx me. In the third week, mere days before my visit, Ashley essentially disappeared. Our system had been for her to call me, hang up, and then I immediately called her back. Sometimes, she would just email me with the time to call. Now all of a sudden, no calls, no emails, and she never seemed to be home when I phoned her.

I sent this email.

```
Subj: What's up?
Date:  September 13, 5:45 PM
From: Vic31
To:  Actingchik84
        It's Wednesday and I'm very excited
seeing you on Saturday. But I'm also nervous
about because you haven't called me for two
days and the conversation before that was,
"I'm tired, so this will be short." I'm not
hitting any panic buttons but my mind is
starting to race a little. I tried to call
you several times last night, but no answer.
```

I received this reply on Thursday.
New York email #15.

```
Subj: (no subject)
Date: September 14, 9:28 PM
From: Actingchik84
To: Vic31
        Hey! Look I have to be honest with you.
The reason I've been being so weird lately and
haven't really wanted to talk is because I am
going through a really rough time with Dean
and he doesn't really like it when I talk to
you. Not that that would stop me, but consid-
ering the circumstances I found it appropri-
ate to keep my phone calls short with you. I
mean it IS his phone, too. And that is why I
may have not seemed very excited about your
visit this weekend. It's just that of course
I want you to come but we CAN NOT fool around
at all. That means we are just FRIENDS.
That's all. I'm sorry but this is what I feel
is right for now. If you don't want to come I
understand but I still would enjoy your com-
pany. I hope you haven't taken this letter
the wrong way. It was not intended to be rude
or anything even close to that. I just had to
let you know before you came. So let me know.
Ashley
```

This was a difficult situation. If she didn't want me there and I went, things would be awkward. But if she did want me there and I refused, it was basically saying, "If I can't get any, then I don't want to be your friend," which wasn't true. In the end, I assumed she still loved me, and, once I arrived in the flesh, things would return to normal. Plus, I'd already told my parents I was heading to New York to see a girl.

Two days later Dad drove me to the train station, his scrotum once again a manageable size. We waited 50 minutes for the train. The ten minutes we were early and the 40 minutes it was late. We both stared out the windshield, quietly listening to the radio. When the train arrived at the depot, Dad said, "Hey. I never told your mom I thought you were gay."

"I didn't figure you had."

"I told her, you *might* be gay."

"Oh. I'm not, you know."

"Yep," he said. "It was just because all of the soul searching and stuff. I just imagine that gay people have to do a lot of soul searching."

"I suppose they probably do," I said, grabbing my backpack. "Thanks for the ride."

THE BIG APPLE
September 17

People seem to have one of two reactions when seeing New York City for the first time. Either, "This is the greatest place on earth," or "Get me the fuck out of here." I went with the latter. I hadn't been in Penn Station five minutes before I wanted on the first train heading west. Ashley was nowhere in sight, and with her strange behavior the past week, I wasn't sure she would show up at all. I took several short, deep breaths, trying to upgrade my condition from scared shitless to merely uncomfortable. Leaning against my backpack, I sat on the floor and closed my tired eyes.

It was my good fortune upon boarding the train back at Waterloo to be seated in a row with no other passengers. I lifted the armrests, stretched out over both seats and could have slept the night away. But some big, fat crybaby had to go and ruin it.

The obese man sitting one row up asked the Amtrak purser if he would have "that person" switch seats with him. My eyes were closed, but I assumed "that person" was me. I didn't move.

"I'm sorry, but he was here first and we can't make him trade with you. If he agrees, be our guest, but Amtrak is not going to ask him."

My only hope was to fake sleep and pray he didn't have the audacity to wake a stranger for an unreasonable favor. Something poked my shoulder. He did have the audacity. Being a sound sleeper, I didn't move. He continued poking, until I roused from my pretend slumber. "What, where the, huh," was my disoriented response to his question. Then right back to phony sleep.

His logic was absurd. He let himself become obese and now wanted special seating privileges. That would be like me getting drunk and demanding that someone in a sleeper car trade me seats. "Why should they lie down? They're sober. I'm drunk. I need it more."

He repeated, "Would you please switch seats with me? I need the room."

Not having the nerve to say, "Tough shit, Fatty," I exchanged seats.

For the next ten hours I sat upright and listened to him snore.

Now, exhausted and abandoned, I sat on the floor of a New York City train station and tried not to come undone. Moments later, Ashley arrived, modeling a T-shirt small enough to expose her newly pierced navel. All of a sudden, New York didn't seem so bad.

Spotting me, she smiled, but it looked forced. "There you are. I was outside smoking a cigarette." She gave me a half-hearted hug, and we walked toward something called the Path Station.

The city was overwhelming. The buildings were so tall and close together I felt caged. The streets were bumper to bumper with cars, and about every third one was a taxi, honking. Unsavory people tried to sell me questionable merchandise as people in suits pushed to get past me.

We descended stairs leading somewhere dark and ominous. Coming from a place with no mass transit, the subways were unnerving. Like walking into an unknown forest at night. Ashley, who had been there all of three weeks, acted like it was the most natural thing in the world.

"Maybe we should just take a cab," I suggested.

"We can't," Ashley said. "I live in Hoboken, which is in New Jersey. We have to take the Path train under the Hudson River."

"The subway goes *under* the river?" I asked.

"It's not the subway, it's the Path train," she said, sounding annoyed by my ignorance.

"Oh, right," I said, having no idea what the difference was.

We each paid a couple dollars at a turnstile and then stood in a platform with three sets of tracks. There was a train waiting on track two.

"Is that our train?" I asked.

"No, we have to wait on track three," she said.

"How do you know which train is ours?"

"See the board lit up by train two? It says Journal Square. Do I live in Journal Square? No. I live in Hoboken. We want the train under the sign that says 'Hoboken' and today it's on track three."

We stood at the track for ten minutes as more people continued to enter the already full platform. The homeless people harmonizing "Lean On Me" were ignored by the other commuters like grit under their feet. Ashley stepped nearer the tracks. "Come on, get up here so we can grab seats." When the train arrived, people pushed to get in position near the doors. When they opened, we raced to sit down. No wonder New

Yorkers are so high-strung. Everything is a competition.

The train was crowded before leaving 33rd Street, and we had four more stops before Hoboken. "How many people do they jam into this thing?"

"A lot," Ashley said, disinterested. "But listen, Dean is really pissed off you're coming. He says he won't speak to you while you're here."

"He is such a baby," I said.

"No, he's just upset. Please, don't be mean to him."

"He can be rude to me, but I have to be nice to him?"

"It's his apartment."

"It's your apartment too, right?"

When the doors of the train finally opened in Hoboken, the people poured out like water through a sieve. Hoboken was an energetic little town. It boasted the most liquor licenses per capita in the country. It seemed to be made up of nothing but bars and restaurants.

"I bet you have a blast here," I said.

"I'm not twenty-one, remember?"

Her apartment was composed of a living room/kitchen area that led to three miniscule bedrooms, all connected. To get to the farthest bedroom you had to pass through the other two. Ashley's was the first one in.

I took a cold shower using the hot water knob, shaved, changed my clothes and Ashley and I set out for Manhattan. She had to work the next day and wanted to help me get my bearings. It was intended as a friendly gesture, but I felt like a bag of kittens about to be tossed out of a car. We never really stopped and looked at anything. Ashley would just say, "This is the Village," and we would kind of walk in silence until she said, "This is Soho, I think," and we kept on moving.

We stopped at a diner for breakfast food. "Have you auditioned for anything yet?" I asked, while buttering my French toast.

"I can't audition until I get head shots," she said. "And I can't afford them right now."

"I thought you saved your money before you got here."

"I did, but that all went into my apartment. My rent is four-fifty a month, and that doesn't count the cable and phone and stuff."

"Still though, even if it was six hundred, divide that three ways, it's still not too bad," I said.

Ashley laughed. "I wish. Four-fifty is my third."

"You guys pay twelve hundred dollars for that piece of shit?" I said.

"Thirteen-fifty, and we were lucky to get it. Housing is expensive out here."

"Won't your parents send you some money for pictures?" I asked.

"Hell no, they don't want me out here in the first place."

"So you moved out here to be an actress, but you can't afford to audition."

"Yeah, I basically moved here to waitress."

"I've got some money," I said. "How much are pictures? Maybe I could loan it to you."

Ashley really considered it for a moment. "I can't let you do that."

"I don't mind. It doesn't make any sense for you to move out here and then not audition."

"I can't, but thanks."

What she could let me do was take her to the theater. She had planned on hitting all the shows on Broadway, but she was too broke to see even one. We taxied to Times Square. Something about the energy of that place made me giddy. I talked non-stop. We passed the Ed Sullivan Theater where David Letterman taped, and I rambled about my favorite Letterman moments. We passed the MTV studio and we talked about music videos. Everything in Times Square was bright and exciting.

My favorite memory of New York was taking Ashley to see *Rent*. She smiled the whole show. Afterward we held hands and walked through Times Square discussing the performance. By the time we got to the 33rd Street station, I felt my old Ashley had returned.

When the train left the Christopher Street stop, a small black man in his late thirties entered our compartment. He wore cheap gray slacks and a white, button-down dress shirt yellowed with age. He carried a clipboard.

"May I have your attention, please? My name is Teddy. I am riding the train all night to collect for the shelter to help feed and clothe the homeless. The money will go for food, milk, clothing and medicine for the homeless. Many of you may not feel like donating because you are not homeless. But maybe just one bad break and you would be without shelter or food. I ask you to please be generous. We do this once a week."

As Teddy said his speech he walked through the compartment and occasionally somebody would hand him a dollar. Most people ignored him, and I wondered how they could all be so selfish.

"Please, even if you give your spare change, it all adds up so the homeless can have a warm meal."

I gave Teddy a five dollar bill when he passed me and he said, "God Bless you, my brother."

It was a little after midnight when we returned to Hoboken. Her roommates were watching television in the living room. Dean sat on the couch staring at the television. When Ashley introduced me he said, "Hey," but never turned. Jamie, a short animated blonde, was much more talkative. She was an aspiring singer and wanted to hear all about *Rent.* Ashley happily explained everything until she remembered Dean off to the side pouting. Her energy dropped, and soon he received all of her attention. Finally speaking, he asked if she would make him a sandwich. The sight of Ashley coddling this trust fund brat disgusted me, and I went to bed. At one point Jamie passed me to get to her room. Dean and Ashley never did.

I had the apartment to myself the next day. It was the first chance I had to look around. Ashley had a few pictures of us, but none were displayed prominently.

Dean's room was laid out like an artist's studio. It had a table with painting supplies on it, some easels supporting canvases and nothing else in terms of furniture. He must have slept on the couch. On the wall were his pictures with Ashley. At the prom, in plays, on Spring Break. The way he used their history to manipulate her disgusted me. Why would Ashley go to all the effort to leave home and then bring along remnants that keep her shackled there?

I was curious as to whether this little prick had any talent, so I removed the cover from one of the canvases. I half expected to see a nude Ashley or something. I shouldn't have been so humble. It turns out that I was the subject. Me, and the horse whose cock I was sucking. At least he gave me the dignity of not doing a mule.

Removing the other cover, I found that Dean's work seemed to have a general theme. In this one, I was being raped by a German shepherd. At least I would like to think it was rape, but the expression on my face could very well be interpreted as consensual. I'm glad art therapy was helping this derelict work through his anger. I would've destroyed the paintings, but I didn't want to give him the satisfaction of knowing that I'd seen them.

The only item on that day's to-do list was to catch the next train home. I knew what was going on here, and it made me mad and broke my heart all at the same time. Unfortunately, the train had already left, so I was stuck in the Big Apple another day. Maybe New York is the greatest city in the world and I was just in the wrong mental state to enjoy it, but being there depressed me. All the times that I'd been alone, didn't compare to the loneliness I felt surrounded by a million people.

After wandering aimlessly through Manhattan, I stumbled across Central Park. I bought a hotdog and a Coke on the outskirts, then entered the park to have my lunch. Sitting a few benches over from me, an old man fed pigeons. It made me think of the goose outside my window. I hadn't changed a bit since then. All this talk about altering my life's course and evolving was bullshit.

Had Kevin been right? Was I here to fail? It didn't feel like that. Ashley was an attractive girl full of passion and life. She was what I wanted. I failed, but it clearly wasn't sabotage. There was no fear of commitment with her. Just because I didn't want to marry Lauren didn't mean I had a problem. Or did it? In the beginning, hadn't she been just as exciting? Why didn't I like her anymore? I couldn't remember.

Three hours later, about to overdose on introspection, I left the park for Times Square. I thought about Ashley and how happy she had been the night before watching *Rent*. She was advancing in the direction of her dreams. Struggling, no doubt, but still endeavoring to live the life she imagined. Right before she moved, Ashley told me that she more than likely would have chickened out if she hadn't met me. That probably should have made me feel better than it did.

It was 10:30 by the time the Path train left the 33rd Street station. Within moments, a man entered in gray pants and a nasty white dress shirt. "May I have your attention please. My name is Teddy. I'm riding the train all night to collect for the shelter to help feed and clothe the homeless..." He gave the exact same speech down to the "I do this once a week" line. Since I hadn't fought hard enough to get a seat I was at a better angle to see his clipboard. It was a blank sheet of paper with random pen marks. It was a scam, but I'll give Teddy credit, he beat the system.

When homeless people on the street asked for money, they were ignored. People didn't want to deal with them personally, but they were willing to give money to someone else who would. The locals knew to ignore him, but there were plenty of visitors, like me the night before, to make it profitable.

Ashley's apartment smelled of eggs when I returned. Ashley was making Dean supper. He sat on the couch pretending to ignore my existence. "How was your day?" Ashley asked me.

"Fantastic!" I said with fake enthusiasm. "I love this city. I want to see everything. I'm going to stay at least another three days. I hope that's okay."

Ashley hesitated a few seconds trying to make eye contact with Dean without me seeing her. "Yeah. Umm, no problem."

"Great. Well, I hope you don't think me rude, but I'm exhausted. I'm going to hit the sack. Feel free to join me if you like." Unable to resist, I turned just before shutting the door. "Night, Dean. I really appreciate you letting me stay."

"Uh, huh," he mumbled.

The next morning I left. I didn't bother to write a note.

PHONE BILL
September 20

When my train arrived at the Waterloo depot, I was lost. I knew I was in Waterloo, but I had no idea what to do with my life. Nothing was working out. Not only was I not happier than before all this started, I was clearly more miserable. My life seemed to have no purpose. There was nothing to look forward to, nothing to accomplish. Everything felt stagnant. What I needed was one positive event to change the luck of my current run. And like a beacon of light, there stood my mother, waiting on the platform.

"You have a hundred and fifty dollar phone bill," she said, handing me the papers to prove it.

I glanced at the phone bill. She had circled any call suspected of being mine. "Okay."

"No. One hundred and fifty dollars is not okay. Who do you keep calling in Fort Wayne?"

"Ashley," I said.

"I thought she lived in New York?"

"She does now," I said. "Are there any New York calls on the bill?"

"There are going to be New York calls!" Apparently they hadn't arrived yet. "You're paying this bill!"

"Of course I am. Now can we please go home?"

I threw my backpack into the car and sat down beside it. Dad sat in the driver's seat. "Your mom has been going crazy over that phone bill."

"So I gathered. I'll write a check when we get back."

Mom buckled herself into the front seat. "You weren't happy, either," she said defensively to Dad.

"No, but as long he pays it, what do I give a shit?" Dad stated.

"What do you give a shit, indeed," Mom repeated. "We're going to have that printed on your tombstone." She turned back to me. "I want that bill paid right away."

"I said I would, and I will," I told her. "I don't have my checkbook on me. So, you're either going to have to wait until we get home or drive me to an ATM."

We drove out of the parking area and almost 30 seconds passed before Mom said again, "I don't like you running up our phone bill."

"What difference does it make, if I pay it?"

"It doesn't," Dad said, putting an end to it.

With the phone bill atrocity solved, or at least put on hold, Mom was free to rattle off her minions of other questions. "Why are you back so early? What happened with that girl? How much longer do you plan on doing nothing with your life?" She never stopped to consider that these subjects might be painful or embarrassing to me. There was always accusation in her voice, like I intentionally plotted against her.

"Listen," I said, "I'm too tired to get into all of this right now."

She grumbled a little but basically let it drop. "Oh, by the way, your friend Wally called. They had their baby."

"Okay," I said, an unhappiness rising within me.

"He wants you to go and see it," she said.

"Okay."

"Are you going to?"

"Eventually, maybe. I'm kind of not in the mood right now." My voice was trembling.

"All of your friends have families now, you know?"

"Yeah, I know." I fought back my tears.

"Are you ever going to get married?" she asked.

"Probably not."

"Why not?"

"Because I'm too fucked up," I yelled. The reservoir broke. If there is anything more pathetic than a 30-year-old man bawling in the back of his parents' car, I haven't seen it...yet.

My parents are good Midwestern people. You would think they would understand the etiquette that applies when a man is crying. You don't look at him. You don't ask him what's wrong. You shut up and pretend not to notice. It's just common courtesy. And you certainly don't do what my mom did next. She turned to me and said, "Tell the truth. Are you gay?"

"GOD DAMN YOU!" I screamed, with all the force my anger and humiliation could project.

She was too shocked to reply. The only words spoken were from Dad, who said quietly, "I *told* you not to mention it."

MICHIGAN
September 21

Late the next morning, I jumped on my motorcycle for a few days of highway therapy. I cruised US 20 west to 131 north through Kalamazoo and Grand Rapids, stopping several times to find shade and get something to drink. It was unseasonably hot for the third week of September.

I particularly enjoyed the stretches of road that cut through farmland as far as the eye could see. It was a beautiful contrast from the overpopulation I had recently experienced. No concrete, no taxis, no yelling. Just soybeans and corn in straight, orderly rows. Farming must be very satisfying. It has a wonderful simplicity. In the spring you bury a seed. You watch a plant grow all summer, then in the fall, God willing, you harvest a crop. They may question the how and what of their daily lives but never why. A farmer knows his purpose. And that's all you could really hope for in life.

The ride was lifting my spirits. On the seat of a motorcycle is my happy place. In my car, I wouldn't have noticed the surroundings or basked in the sun's warm glow. On a bike things are experienced differently. If it's hot, I sweat. If it's raining, I get wet. Me and nature, in it together. Plus, I have a keener awareness of mortality. No matter whose fault the accident is, if I get hit by a car, I'm screwed. So I key in on those around me. Does this guy see me? Will he stop? And this focus on the moment melts away the anxiety.

In Cadillac, Michigan I accidentally got off of 131 north and wound up on 55 east. Since there was no particular place I was heading, I didn't correct my error. It didn't matter where I went. It just felt good to be free. The challenge is to live my life like this when I'm not on my motorcycle. To find serenity in my environment all of the time, to allow myself to be led.

A few uneventful hours passed, then without warning, my bike made a moaning sound and lurched. Apparently the shit storm, which currently was my life, had no intention of letting up. At 6:00 p.m., barreling down US 27 at 70 miles per hour, my motorcycle completely lost power. I couldn't believe it. *Et tu, Bikey?* At 45 miles per hour, I veered onto the shoulder and coasted to a stop.

The engine quit. I hit the ignition button, nothing. I checked the gas. A quarter of a tank left, more than enough. For the next several minutes I sat on the bike and watched traffic buzz passed me at high speeds. I had no idea what to do.

The bike was too heavy to push, so my options were limited. Either leave it and walk to the nearest town (I had no idea where that was), or wait and hope a cop would drive by and help me. I hadn't seen a state patrol car all afternoon. I tried to start the bike again. It wouldn't fire, but it did turn over several times. I decided to wait another ten minutes and then try again.

Exactly eight minutes and 22 seconds later (my watch was set to the chrono mode), an old, beat-up Ford truck pulled off the road in front of me. The bed of this half-ton was filled with scrap metal. A mangy blue-tick heeler barked inside the cab. A big man got out of the truck and walked toward me. He removed his green John Deere hat to wipe his brow with an oily rag pulled from the back pocket of his grimy cut-off jean shorts. He was shirtless, but his sunburned arms and neck contrasted enough with his lily-white torso to create the illusion that he wore one.

"You gotcha a bike problem here?" he asked, when he approached me. I could smell the stink off this guy at three feet. A potpourri of grease, dirt and sweat.

"It stopped running. I think it might have overheated."

"How long you been sittin' here?"

"Almost thirty minutes."

"An' it still won't start?" He scratched his hairy belly and thought. "Thirty minutes, I don't know. I reckon it should start. But then again," he said looking over the bike, "I don't know nothin' about these foreign engines."

"Ten minutes ago, it turned over a little," I said.

"Well, try her again, if she don't start I'll give you a ride to town. That is, if you don't mind dogs."

Oh sweet Lord. Start you son-of-a-bitch, start.

I hit the ignition button. The bike kept turning over, "hm, hm, hm, hm, hm, hm, hm, hm, hm, hm, hm, hm..."

"Give her a little gas," the man yelled.

I did. The bike fired. "Vroom, vroom."

Even though the engine was running, the bike had little power. It topped out at 30 miles per hour. Fortunately the man offered to follow me to the next exit just in case. What a good guy, taking time out of his day to help a stranger. Despite the smell and admittedly rough appearance, he's a better man than I, who never stops, even though I have no job or anything else to get to. A lot of times I've considered helping, but fear they've pulled over in some cleverly disguised ruse to rob me.

The man honked and pointed out his window to the Rosebush town exit. Sputtering up the ramp I waved good-bye. *Fare thee well, my noble hillbilly. Angel of the highway.*

Rosebush was a small town with no hotels, so after fueling up, I still had to drive eight miles to Mt. Pleasant. For whatever reason, with a full tank, the bike ran better. Still cautious, however, I didn't push the bike any harder than 50. After passing a sign that indicated Mt. Pleasant was two miles away; I throttled up to 65. No problems. Minutes later I checked into the Mt. Pleasant Holiday Inn, much relieved.

BO
September 21

After a hot shower and a delivered pizza, I walked down to the hotel bar for a nightcap. To my surprise the place was packed with young, attractive women. I mean like 40 or 50 of them. And even though there were some young men chasing them around, the women outnumbered the men three to one. I sat down at the bar and ordered a bottle of Coors Light.

A man who looked younger than me, but dressed more grown up, sat to my right. I asked him, "Why are all these kids at a Holiday Inn? Is there a conference or something?"

"They all go to Central Michigan," he said. "Mt. Pleasant doesn't give them a ton of options. Tonight is four dollar pitchers, so they all come here to get drunk."

The bartender handed me my beer. "Two-seventy-five," he said. When he walked away, I said to the guy next to me, "That bastard should have told me about the cheap pitchers." I dropped three dollars and tipped him nothing other than the quarter.

The guy slapped his khaki pants and grinned. The pitcher in front of him was nearly empty. "You here on business?" he asked.

"Just traveling," I told him. "I still can't believe how many girls are here."

There was no band, no karaoke, just a DJ playing CDs that only a handful of girls danced to. "Every Wednesday, like clock work. I actually plan around it," he told me. Tim was there on business. He was a sales rep for Gillette.

"The razors and shit?" I asked.

"Yeah," he laughed, "the razors and shit."

"I use Gillette razors, but they scratch my face up." I told him.

This sparked a fifteen-minute discussion on the fact that I used the older razor and should switch over to the new one. Then the conversation veered to what a great company Gillette was, and their wonderful

401 K plan, company cars and on and on and on. Tim couldn't have met another man who cared less than me, but he was young and it was probably still all very exciting to him, so I listened. Plus, having him to talk with kept me from being the weird guy alone at the bar.

"I'll get the next round," he told me. "I'm on the company teat, tonight. You know, away on business."

"I remember those days," I said, and left it at that.

Tim asked me what I did, and when I said "nothing" he had questions. I could tell he was the type of person who wouldn't understand. He wore a gold watch. He carried a wad of cash in his platinum money clip. This was a guy who defines himself through career and possessions. That's fine, but I wasn't going to waste my time trying to explain myself. "It's kind of a sore subject," I told him.

"Gotcha," he said. "I wouldn't tell the ladies though if I were you. Central Michigan is a liberal arts college. A lot of girls here with unemployable majors just trying to marry well."

"You ever picked up a girl here?"

"Not yet. They all seem to have their little cliques."

I looked around the room. "You see those two girls sitting over at that table?" I pointed to an Asian and a redhead drinking beer and smoking cigarettes. They were laughing about something.

Tim looked and made some "guy" comment.

"I've been watching them," I said. "I think they might be here alone. I haven't seen any guys around them, and neither one ever looks at the door. So I'm guessing they aren't meeting anyone either."

"You want to go talk with them?" he asked.

"I don't see why not. Let's get a pitcher of beer and take it over there."

Tim ordered the beer. I observed the girls. They were both pretty, but I was drawn to the Asian. She had a pleasant way about her that seemed inviting. She also happened to have incredible legs sprouting out of a short black skirt, which she kept crossing and uncrossing.

After Tim paid for the pitcher we approached the girls. Of course we could join them. They were roommates. The redhead was Daphne. The Asian was Bo. We talked as a group for a few minutes, but soon broke off into smaller discussion groups. Tim and Daphne in one. Bo and I in the other.

Bo was 23 and a junior at Central Michigan. She had jumped around from college to college, and her major now was general studies. She didn't worry about things like finding a job. She wasn't even sure if she would work directly after graduation. Bo had rich parents who seemed to indulge her indifference toward responsibility.

Ignoring Tim's advice, I told Bo about quitting my job to figure things out. "I think that's awesome, you know," she said. "Who cares about money and jobs, really? That stuff is so boring."

"I totally agree," I said.

"I just want to live a happy, interesting life," she said. "I want a fun husband someday and a job I love to do. I don't care about anything else."

"I want to find a woman I love. Really love, you know. A girl who makes me laugh and doesn't bitch about the little stuff."

Bo wanted to play a game where we would ask each other questions. She went first. "If you could meet anybody from anytime, who would it be?"

I thought about this and said, "Probably Jesus. I would love to know his opinion on organized religion."

"That's a good answer," she said.

"Yeah, Jesus or the first guy who ever ate an oyster."

"The first guy to eat an oyster?" She made a face.

"Sure. I'd like to know his opinion on organized religion." Bo smiled. Talking to her was more than just comfortable. It was fun. I actually felt giddy. "Now let me ask you a question. Which would you prefer? To be a creative genius and know how great you are, but you die penniless and misunderstood. Or be completely weak, yet rich and famous."

"Ooh, that's tough. I don't know if I can answer that. What would you pick?"

"I'd be mediocre and successful. The world is full of people like that. As long as I knew it, so I didn't act like a pretentious ass, I'd be okay with it. Who wants to be frustrated their whole life?"

Bo started to ask another question, but I stopped her. "Wait a minute. You didn't answer the last one. So I get to ask you another one. Let me think." While thinking I could hear Tim talking. He told Daphne that he was buying a house because, you know, he's got plenty of money, and it's a good investment. As he discussed realtors and resale value,

Daphne just kept saying "uh, huh…uh, huh." Tim didn't have a clue.

Bo uncrossed her legs and then crossed them again with the opposite leg on top. Her foot was just inches from me. This put body parts in my mind, so I asked, "What is your favorite physical quality in a man?"

"That's easy. The butt," she said. "He's got to have a nice ass." That didn't bode well for me and my skinny bum. "And tall," she said. "I love tall guys." That was more encouraging.

Daphne, sick of talking with Tim, asked what we were talking about. "Nothing," Bo said, implying that we wanted to be left alone. We had a great rhythm going, and neither of us wanted to ruin it by rejoining the foursome. Daphne stared at her like, "My guy sucks, so talk to me." Bo waved her off with her hand. Her face was, "My guy is good, so take one for the team." Poor Daphne. Lucky me.

Bo, turning her attention away from the others, asked me, "If you could have any super power, what power would you pick?"

"Hmmm," I said, thinking. "I'm not sure."

"I know mine," she said. "Invisibility. Then I could sneak into rooms and hear what people said behind my back."

"No way. If people dislike me, I'd just as soon not know."

"Then what power would you pick?" she asked again.

"I'm not even sure what powers there are to choose from," I said. She told me to just think of Superman. "I always thought Superman was kind of a bullshit hero," I told her. "*Because* of all those powers. He had super strength. He was bullet proof. He could see through buildings. *And* he could fly. It's too much. Why not just make him all-knowing and be done with it? Now Batman, that's a plausible-"

"Just pick one," Bo said.

I thought about it for a moment. "Bullet-proof," I said. "Because if nobody can hurt you, there's nothing to be afraid of. Think about it. It wouldn't be scary to be lost in a big city. If some bully picked on you at a bar, you wouldn't even care, because there's nothing he can do injure you."

"Technically, if you were just bullet-proof, and didn't have the super human strength, you could still be raped, right?" Bo grinned at the devaluing of my super power.

"Yes, technically, you still could be raped. But I've seen some bar fights and I'm pretty sure the bouncers would step in at that point."

I thought of another good question. "If you could marry a really good looking guy who was horrible in bed, or a really ugly guy who was great in bed, which would it be? All else equal."

"That's more of a guy's question," she said. "Women don't care as much about looks."

"That's true," I said, "plus, it's harder for a guy to be good at sex. The size issue, the duration, men have a lot more things that could be amiss." Bo agreed with that statement, and I rephrased my question so the guy who was good in bed was socially embarrassing. And good-looking was amended to a perfect match in every other way.

Bo thought for a moment, "That's tough, because you're talking about marriage. That's pretty permanent and good sex is very important to me." While thinking, Bo crossed her legs again. She had to be doing that on purpose. "I would take the perfect match guy and train him sexually before we got married."

"What if you couldn't train him, what if he had a tiny penis?"

"Then he's history," she said.

"Wow. That's a little cold."

"Are you worried?" she asked.

"Nah," I said. "It's the nice ass thing that has me nervous. If we got married would you force me to get buttock implants?"

"Of course not," she said. "I'm not that shallow. I'd rather have you spend the money buying me presents."

When the bartender yelled for last call, Bo said, "It's too early to go home." Tim and I agreed. Daphne was silent on the matter.

We left the lounge and stood in front of the pool area. A sign read no admission after nine o'clock. "Why don't we sit in the hot tub?" I suggested.

"It's locked," Daphne said, holding her car keys. "Plus, we don't even have our bathing suits."

"We can just climb the fence," Bo said. She was up and over the fence before Daphne finished saying, "Bo, don't."

I followed. Daphne and Tim did not.

Soaking her feet in the hot tub was pretty easy for Bo. She just had to kick off her shoes and put her feet in. It was more difficult for me. I had to remove my Doc Martens, my socks, then take off my jeans. Bo, however made it worth my while. Once I sat down beside her, she rubbed her bare foot against mine in the water. I put my arm around her back and rubbed her thigh. Receiving no resistance, I kissed her. We made out by the hot tub for several minutes. Each moment gathering our courage. It quickly escalated from kissing to a full-body grope.

I paused for a moment, "Bo," I said. "Let me ask you a really important question."

"Okay," she said, hesitantly.

"Now don't answer right away," I told her. "I want you to think for a few minutes."

"What is it?" she asked.

"If VH1 was going to do a show on Guns-N-Roses, would it be *Behind the Music* or *Legends*?"

Bo laughed at the absurdity of the question, then answered. "I would have to say *Legends*, if for no other reason than the things I experienced in middle school listening to *Sweet Child O' Mine*."

"I like you even more now," I told her. While kissing, Bo guided me out of the hot tub and slammed me against the cold tile. Quickly, I discovered that she was not wearing a skirt after all, but a pair of skorts. Shorts that look like a skirt, which were removed as she slithered up my body. Lying on my back I felt her smooth thighs on each side of my face.

Clearing his throat, a middle-aged security guard opened the door. Bo was too busy to notice until I tapped her, and pointed. Bo ran off to find her clothes. To force the security guard to look at me, instead of bottomless Bo, I said, "What? We're not allowed to sit in the hot tub?"

After being escorted from the pool area, we found Daphne sitting alone in the foyer. "That was totally uncalled for," Daphne said to Bo. "I wasn't interested in Tim at all, and you left me alone with him to go sit on this guy's face."

Bo blushed. "You saw that?"

"Uh, yeah." Daphne was disgusted.

"I like him," Bo said.

"Obviously," Daphne retorted. "Come on, let's go."

I followed the ladies to their car. As Daphne started the car, Bo and I stood outside. "I have my motorcycle here, if you'd like to go for a ride."

"I love motorcycles," she said. "As long as it's not a sports bike. Those things suck." I was falling in love with this girl. Bo opened the car door, "Hey, Vic's taking me for a motorcycle ride. I'll see you tomorrow."

Daphne said, "Whatever," and drove off.

After some more kissing, we walked to my motorcycle. "You don't like sports bikes, huh?" I asked, proud not to be a sports-bike guy.

"No way, man. I only ride Harleys," she said.

"You realize that this is a Honda."

"Yeah, right."

"No, I'm serious," I said. "Read the gas tank."

She read the gas tank out loud, "Honda Shadow. Well, I can't ride this then." I laughed. But she didn't. "I'm serious. I can't."

"What are you talking about?"

"I do have a reputation in this town," she said.

"You couldn't even tell the difference," my voice raised to a squeaky pitch.

Bo laughed hard. "I'm kidding. Come on. You believed me?" She laughed again. "Yeah, I'll let you go down on me," she said, mocking herself, "but I won't ride your bike."

"I didn't think you could be serious," I said, now appreciating the joke. "I mean you, of all people, not riding a Honda."

Bo stopped laughing. "What do you mean, me of all people?"

She wasn't kidding about this. "I, uh, just thought you were too classy to be a hard-core-"

"Because I'm Asian, I can't like Harley's?"

"No. No. Of course not," I said, stalling for a lie. None coming to me, I added quite unwisely, "You have to admit, it would be a little ironic."

"Oh my God! You're an idiot! I'm Korean. Honda is from Japan," she said, too loudly for my comfort.

"Honda isn't Korean?" I asked in a desperate effort to save the situation.

"Maybe it's Chinese," she said. "What's the difference? We all have squinty little eyes." She walked away from me.

"Don't go," I said running after her. "I'm sorry."

"Just leave me alone," she said, more annoyed than angry.

I had no idea why this was so distasteful to her. It may have been a stupid thing to say, but obviously it wasn't based on hate. Maybe it had to do with a previous incident in her life that she has never fully recovered from. Maybe she was drunk. It didn't really matter at this point. I had to undo this damage quick before I lost her. "Bo. Don't. I really, really like you. Don't let one stupid comment mess this whole thing up."

She reached into her purse had grabbed mace. "Get away from me or I will pepper spray your ass." I continued to follow her. "I'm serious," she yelled.

"Can I at least have your phone number, so we can talk about this later?"

"Fuck off!" she yelled.

"So that's it? Those are the last words you'll ever say to me?"

"No." She turned back to me. "These are the last words I'll ever say to you. Hondas are for pussies!"

CHEMICAL IMBALANCE
September 24

Mom was pouring milk shakes out of a blender when I came home from my afternoon ride. The past few days since returning from Michigan, she had been especially nice to me, even making my favorite meals.

After she filled all three glasses, I reached for one. "That's not yours," she said, handing me a different one.

"What makes the difference?"

"It doesn't," she said. "Just take this one."

"What's going on here?"

"Nothing," she insisted.

I sniffed it. It smelled all right, but still I was suspicious. "Let me see you take a drink of it." Mom took a drink. "No, with a straw," I said. "The poison might be in the bottom."

"For heaven's sakes." She grabbed a straw and took another drink. "Satisfied?"

I was. I sipped my shake. It was good. I took a big drink. Something gritty and bitter entered my mouth. Noticing the face I made, Mom asked, "What's wrong?"

"I think there's something in this."

Mom grabbed the shake out my hand and drank from it. "No, it's fine."

I took another sip. The same gritty texture. "Yuck. There's something in this."

"Oh, there is not," Mom said.

I grabbed a different shake. "That's your dad's." I took a sip. It was fine. I took another big drink. Again, no problem. I grabbed the third shake. "You can't drink all three," Mom yelled. After a couple of drinks I determined that only mine had that gritty texture.

"What did you put in my shake?"

"Nothing." She walked away carrying the other two glasses to the table.

Looking around the counter, I spotted a large bottle of St. John's wort. "Ah ha!" I picked up the bottle and shook it. "What's this?"

Mom knew she was busted. "I'm just trying to help you. You need to be taking something."

"I don't need anti-depressants."

"Don't be stubborn. It's ridiculous that you're miserable. You have a chemical imbalance. These drugs will get you back to normal."

"I'm fine."

"Crying in the car?" She lifted her palms and cocked her head. I had no answer. While pulling the baked beans out of the oven she said, "It's not your fault. You have a chemical imbalance."

"Would you stop saying that?"

"We've made an appointment for you with a therapist."

"What!"

"Don't worry, we're paying for it."

"I'm not going."

The door opened and Dad entered carrying a plate of barbecued chicken. Molly scurried in behind at his feet.

"Yes, you are!" Mom said.

"No, I'm not!"

"You're not doing what?" Dad asked.

"Going to a therapist," I said.

To Mom he said, "I told you he'd taste those pills."

"He's got to do something," Mom said. "He's got a chemical imbalance."

Dad and I sat down at the table for dinner. Mom pulled three baked potatoes out of the oven, then joined us. Dad stared at his shake. "You didn't put any shit in mine did you?"

"I put diet pills in yours," Mom said.

"I'm serious," Dad said.

"Me too."

Dad's eyes narrowed as he looked at his shake. Apparently the reward was worth the risk and he took a small sip. He smacked his lips together. Then took a big drink.

"I put a laxative in it," Mom said. Dad spit it out. "I'm just kidding," she said, laughing sadistically. "There's nothing in it."

"God damn you," Dad said. Mom couldn't stop laughing. "You're the one who needs the therapy."

"You're appointment is next week at the Family Wellness Clinic in Auburn," Mom said turning her attention back to me.

"I'm not going."

"Ray, tell him," Mom said. Dad gave Mom a dirty look. Back to me, Mom said, "At least go to a doctor and get some Prozac."

I had smothered my baked potato with beans and was taking a big bite. "No."

"You won't go to therapy. You won't get anti-depressants."

"That's right."

There was a pause. Then a deep sigh. "When are you going to Europe?" Mom asked.

"I don't know, for sure."

"Maybe you should go pretty soon," she said.

The plane tickets were purchased the next day.

FOOL'S PARADISE
September 30

I met Denny back at The Castle for a Fort Wayne celebrity softball game. Local radio and television personalities, as well as a few former in-state college athletes all gathered to help raise money for the local food bank. Denny found this event to be more about feeding egos than the hungry, but when they asked him to dance, he agreed. With the Wizards season ending almost a month ago, he felt this would be a good tune-up before hockey season started. But he couldn't have cared less about the high jinks on the field. What he did seem to be concerned with were my travel plans.

"What are you going to Europe for?" he asked.

"I don't know, to see it," I replied.

Denny tapped his fingers on his belly. "Let me guess? You're not taking a tour are you?"

"No. I'm backpacking."

Denny shook his head with disdain. "Why not take the tour? You'll see more, and it probably isn't much more expensive."

"I don't know. I want the adventure."

"No," Denny retorted. "You just want to be able to say you did it. You're going to turn into one of those pretentious jerks who prattle on at parties about when he backpacked through Europe. You'll see all the sites. 'Oh the Louvre, it's great.' You'll say. 'The Coliseum, just splendid.'"

The hotdog vendor walked by. He never even bothered to ask if Denny wanted a hotdog. He just handed him two. Denny handed me a dog, and I covered it with mustard.

Denny continued his rant, "Honestly, backpacking through Europe is just so cliché. The same with riding your motorcycle all over the country."

"Hey, I love my motorcycle!"

"I know you do, but it's just getting to be too much. Motorcycles, backpacking through Europe. Why don't you start carrying around a sketch pad, and wearing a beret. It would be no less ridiculous."

"Dude, I've always dreamed of backpacking through Europe. I never had the time or the money. Now I do."

"So go. Then come back and bore everybody with pictures and stories of cathedrals that are older than the United States. Maybe even write a wry travel journal, full of insights about how we really don't have any history in this country. That hasn't been overdone yet."

"Maybe I will," I told him.

"Definitely. You should." He took a bite of hotdog. "Then become an expert on wine. That would be perfect. Over dinner you could make catty little comments belittling the wine selection in Fort Wayne restaurants. Then go on a diatribe about the difference between wine and champagne, or which wine goes with which meal."

"That would be perfect; I think I shall," I said. I might have taken this conversation more seriously if Denny hadn't been wearing a homemade Wizards uniform with his baseball cap on backwards. "At least I'll have seen the shit," I told him. "You never leave Fort Wayne."

"That's because I don't run from my problems," he said.

"I'm not running from my problems. I'm just seeing what's out there."

"Out there. Your problems aren't out there. They're in you. You act like you're the only person who has ever been searching for answers. But you don't even know what you're searching for, do you?"

"I know," I told him.

"What then?" he demanded.

"I'm trying to find what I want to do with my life."

"Guess again, String Bean," he said. "You're looking for happiness."

"No shit," I said. "We're all looking for happiness."

"If you're so smart, then why do you keep looking in the wrong places?" he asked.

"There's no happiness in Europe?" I laughed.

"Not for you, there won't be. And if there is, it'll be fleeting. Because happiness is always in the moment, and you don't live in the moment. You try to relive your past or you fantasize about the future, but until you accept today you aren't going to be happy."

At that point the radio team retired the side, and Denny stood up to start stretching. He would be making a public ass of himself as soon as the inning was over.

"You're exaggerating. People go to Europe every day and believe it or not, some of them are happy," I told him.

"Let me tell you something, my friend. Emerson said that traveling is a fool's paradise. You'll dream of Naples and think that you'll become intoxicated with its beauty and lose your sadness. But when you get to Naples it will still be your same sad self, identical as to who you fled from here."

"I'm not even going to Naples," I told him.

"Naples isn't the point!" he screamed.

I don't know what was funnier to me, watching him get all bent out of shape, or seeing the dirty looks mothers gave him for yelling.

"You know what else Emerson said?" I asked, my voice low, so not to be heard by the neighboring children.

"What?" He grabbed his ankle and stretched it behind him.

"He said that any pussy can have big ideas when they hide in their mother's basement, but it's a great man who has the balls to go out in the world and live those ideals."

"Emerson said that?" Denny asked, doubting my source.

"I'm paraphrasing," I said.

"Oh really," Denny whispered. "Emerson didn't say 'any pussy can have big ideas?'"

"No, that part was accurate. It was the rest I couldn't remember."

The short stop for the radio team hit into a double play ending the inning. The music played for the seventh inning stretch. The crowd cheered in anticipation of Denny's performance.

"Don't you think it's ironic that you lecture me on integrity and looking inside myself, and you're about to dance on a dug out," I said, perhaps cruelly.

"The fact that you find irony in it only goes to show that it's partially your ignorance that keeps you from finding inner peace," Denny said, then danced his fat ass off to "Staying Alive" by the Bee Gee's.

EUROPE
October 6

The stubby brick of a woman stared at me. Most of the time I could glance away and pretend not to notice, but this time our eyes met. I forced a smiled. She returned it, waiting to be engaged in conversation. But I couldn't, or more accurately didn't. Her mere presence irritated me. She fiddled with the little diamond on her left ring finger. It would've been rude not to say something though. I cleared my throat. She smiled at me again.

Our train shook as it pulled out of the Amsterdam station exactly on time. For a moment I peeped out of the window, watching our passage from indoors to out. No windmills, no wooden shoes, just a lot of really tall, blonde people.

I turned my attention back to my compartment and the intrusion across from me. "You been enjoying Europe so far?"

"It's nice," she said.

"Do you have a favorite spot?"

"I don't know. Maybe Paris."

"Why's that?" I asked.

"I guess the churches."

Well, I tried. Standing up, I reached into the overhead luggage bin and removed a sheet from my backpack. Often on this trip I'd be staying in hostels, which offer no bedding. A travel guide recommended sewing a sheet together like a sleeping bag. They called it a sleep sack.

We were alone for the moment in the six-seat compartment. I sat in the seat nearest to the window, facing the direction we traveled. She sat in the middle seat opposite of me with an embarrassed smile on her face. With her hands folded in her lap, she tried not to look uncomfortable in the midst of our awkward silence.

Kicking off my blue Nikes, I stepped into the sheet and stretched out across the aisle. Eyes closed, hands behind my head, unavailable.

The compartment door slid open and the woman's husband

entered. A scrawny little guy whose gingham shirt was too baggy and whose jeans were too tight. He returned from the snack car with a small bag of fruit. He sat down beside his wife and handed her a banana. He threw an apple at me. It bounced off my chest and into my lap.

"Ouch, you dumb ass. That hurt." As good friends often do, he laughed at my pain. The first leg of my backpacking adventure would be spent with my old college roommate, Pea, whom I hadn't seen in like forever, and his wife, Cindy, whom I barely knew.

I tossed the apple back to Pea. "I'm too tired to eat it." It had been a long couple of days. My flight itinerary was Fort Wayne to Pittsburgh. Pittsburgh to Philadelphia. Philly to London. London to Amsterdam. I had been in the Netherlands just under two hours before we boarded the train.

"You could have just flown to Venice, you know," Pea said, wiping the yellow delicious on his shirt. "Why didn't you?"

The lie I told Pea was, "I wanted more time to spend with you." The truth was, I'm a tremendous coward who is terrified of being stranded alone in Italy.

"Have I seen you since our wedding?" Pea asked.

"I don't remember. Have you?"

"I'm pretty sure that's the only time we ever met," Cindy added, holding more peel than banana.

"That was like two years ago," Pea said. "Time sure does get away from you."

"What's new, anything?" I asked.

"I'm going to grad school and living in Holland," Pea almost sang it, reinforcing that everything is new, you dumb-ass. What a stupid question. Purdue University sends me to the Netherlands to study swine production for my master's thesis, and you want to know if anything is new. Duh!

"I was surprised to hear you weren't farming anymore." In four years of college Pea never once entertained the notion of any other career. No internships. No summer jobs. College was just someplace he went to learn a couple of things, maybe, and find a wife, hopefully.

"Between my dad and uncles there wasn't enough room." Cindy held his hand, consoling him. "And we couldn't afford to buy more land because of urban sprawl." Pea's face turned bitter. "These old farmers are making a killing selling off their land for residential plots."

"I don't know where the food is going to come from in twenty years," Pea's wife added, equally bitter.

"Cindy's from a farm, too."

She looked like a farm girl. Short, thick and built for hard work. Bred from stock that appreciated practicality over extravagance.

"Her family had grand champion beef at the fair three different years," Pea stated. A proud little smile formed on his face.

I yawned, then apologized for it. "Is that where you met Pea?"

"Who?" Cindy asked.

"Vic used to call me Pea in college." She looked at him strangely.

"I sort of knew David from 4-H," emphasis on the David. "But he's five years older than me, so we didn't think of each other like that back then." Cindy laughed at the scandal of it all. "Have you ever dated a girl five years younger?"

"I sure haven't lately." My eyes were getting heavy. I needed to wrap this up.

"Your girlfriend's my age, right?" Pea, who was a year younger than me, had apparently not been filled in on my current life's track.

"Actually Pea, I sort of broke up with that one about the same time I quit my job."

"What?" Apparently, Pea hadn't heard the news.

"I sold my house and moved back in with my parents, too." I laid back into the seat, hands under my head like a pillow.

Pea's eyes bulged. "Why would you do that?"

"I'm not really sure." Huge yawn. "It's either God's work, fear of commitment, or a chemical imbalance."

None of that mattered now, though. I was in Europe. In my mind, traveling abroad was going to be an Impressionist painting, full of sunflowers and water lilies. Soon I would be sipping absinthe, meeting interesting strangers and talking about art. I allowed myself a smile as slumber overtook me.

I drifted in and out of sleep for the next three hours but could never find a position that suited me. I was too tall to lie across the seats like a bed. My feet had to remain on the floor, twisting my back. Sitting up caused my neck to ache. The most comfortable position was leaning forward with my face on my knees, but one can only sit so long with your nose at your crotch before it starts to feel like a punishment.

For 15 minutes I watched passing city lights reflect off Pea's head as he slept. I almost didn't recognize the guy anymore. In the past 24 months, his hair had receded to the point where describing him as "balding" or "bald" was entirely a matter of generosity. He looked 40 years old.

Pea sat with his arm around Cindy. For pillows she used Pea's shoulder; he used her head. They looked comfortable against one another. That's when it hit me. *You're all alone. Life is passing you by.* The heaviness. Welcome to fool's paradise. Different land, same sad me. Must...find...distraction. I kicked Pea in the foot.

"What? What is it?" Pea said, rubbing his eyes.

"Hey, what's the word for when two words sound the same but mean something different?" I asked.

Pea stared straight ahead and closed his eyes tight like he was trying to adjust his contacts with his eyelids. He opened his eyes to find me still waiting for an answer. "I don't know. 'Onomatopoeia', maybe?"

"No. That's not right," I said. "Onomatopoeia is when a word sounds like what it means, you know like plop or buzz. What I'm talking about is when two words sound alike but are different. I can't bear that bare ass bear."

"You lost me," Pea said as he checked his watch. It was a little after 11:00 p.m.

"There's a word, om, omoly, omniv-"

"Omnivorous," Pea said. He kept his voice low.

"Is that even a word?" I asked.

More deep blinking from Pea, then a yawn. "It means being everywhere at once, I think."

"First of all, you moron, that's omnipotent. Secondly, if you don't think it means words that sound alike then why would you say it?" Another yawn from Pea. I pressed forward. "Come on think, the fly tried to fly into my fly."

Cindy raised her head. "It's homonym. Two words that sound alike but are different are homonyms." She grabbed Pea's wrist and looked at his watch, then laid her head back down.

"That sounds right," I stated. "How'd you know that?"

"I'm omniscient," she said without opening her eyes. "And I also eat both meat and vegetables."

Looking to Pea I mouthed "What?" He shrugged his shoulders and mouthed, "She reads books."

"My point is, Pea, that re-seed and recede both are words that sound alike. But to *re-seed* your lawn means that something that once was bare will now grow something. And if your hair is *receding* it means that what once grew something is now bare. Don't you find that ironic?"

"This is what you woke me up for?" Pea asked.

"Seriously, don't you think it's funny?"

"Yeah," Pea said, "It's fricking hilarious."

His "fricking" derailed my train of thought. "When did you start saying fricking?"

"What's wrong with fricking?" Pea's little act of ignorance didn't fool me. He knew how annoying it was to listen to someone actively not cussing with those little mutations of the real word. Frick, fudge, dang, gosh darn, crap, cheese and rice. Pea was reminded of my policy, which quickly summed up is, you either say the profanity or nothing at all.

"David doesn't cuss anymore," Cindy stated.

"He doesn't," I said, unable to stifle my laughter. In the old days, Pea was a connoisseur of foul language. It was how his soul expressed itself. I knew a ban against the curses had to drive him nuts.

"No, he doesn't," Cindy repeated.

"What about 'fugging' then? That at least *sounds* like the word."

"Let's drop it," Pea said.

I laughed again and pointed at him with both index fingers, like a child behind their mother's back. Pea glanced down to make sure that Cindy's eyes were closed, then flipped me the bird.

VENICE
October 7

It was in large part my fault we didn't have lodging secured when we arrived in Venice Saturday morning. Nothing on this trip, with the exception of the destination, would be pre-planned. Life can't lead you if you're following an itinerary.

Descending the steps of the train station, we were approached by an American man in his early 20s wearing moccasins and baggy cotton pullstring pants. He smelled like a dirty sidewalk.

"Do you have room reservations anywhere?" he asked. Pea stared at the ground, refusing to speak or even make eye contact. Cindy answered his question. Pea cast her an evil glance.

"They're aren't any rooms available in Venice, but we have some cabins left at the campsite," he told us. We could make reservations now, store our backpacks, and take a bus to the site that evening.

Pea walked away from the young man without ever looking at him. He was visibly annoyed when Cindy and I didn't move, waving us over.

"Maybe we should talk about it and get back to you," I suggested.

"Fine. I'm not trying to pressure you or anything, but it will probably fill up tonight, beings as there is, you know..." he stammered with his words.

"No rooms in all of Venice," Pea finished his thought from the distance.

The young man sensed Pea's skepticism. "Hey man, I'm not trying to rip you off or anything." He sounded like a California surfer.

"We know," Cindy assured him. "Give us a moment, please." She seemed shy at first, but quickly into the trip became more assertive, especially when decisions needed to be made.

We congregated on the steps between the train station and the canal. Putting our packs down, we surveyed the city. Tourists floated by on gondolas, enjoying the sunny day and beautiful backdrop that is Venice. "Why were you so rude to that guy?" Cindy asked Pea.

"Maybe we should head back to the train station and make reservations at that campground."

"I agree," Cindy said.

"I don't want to go back now, we're clear on the other side of town," Pea threw his bag down. "Let's rest first." It was muggy, and Pea's forehead was glistening.

"What's the matter, Pea?" I asked. "You out of shape?"

"Believe me, I'm in as good of shape as you are."

"Then why are you the only one who wants to rest?"

"Because I'm the only one carrying two people's stuff." Pea and Cindy only owned one large pack, so the majority of their clothes were being lugged around by Pea. Cindy had a smaller bag stuffed as full as possible, but it really didn't compare with the weight he had to carry.

"Switch me bags," Cindy told Pea. "I'll carry it for a while." Pea refused to hear of it, but in reality, she was probably better suited. Her shoulders were broader, and her legs were stronger. Although Pea had put on some weight after marriage, most of it had gone to his gut. He was still mostly elbows, knees and Adam's apple.

We relented and allowed Pea a five-minute break. "David, you're apologizing to that guy when we get back," Cindy said to Pea while we filled our water bottles at a drinking fountain.

"I am not," Pea said. He scratched at his thigh furiously with his left hand.

"Oh yes you are," she stated firmly. "And you better pray that there's a cabin left."

"There'll be fricking cabins left," Pea shouted.

"Fugging," I corrected.

"Would you shut the fuck up?"

"David!" Cindy barked.

"Aahhh!" Pea shook two fists in the air.

"Come on, let's go."

"I'm not ready yet." Pea had decided to be stubborn.

"Tough, we're going." Cindy stuffed the little bag into his chest. She was carrying the big pack, gosh darn it! At five foot two, Cindy was more than a foot shorter than I was, but I wouldn't want to tangle with her. She was one tough little hobbit.

"Because he's running a fricking scam," Pea said tensely.

"Fugging," I corrected. It was ignored.

"Maybe he's telling the truth," Cindy said.

"Come on," Pea insisted. "It's not the busy season anymore. He expects me to believe that there's nothing in all of Venice...in October." In Pea's mind, four months in Europe qualified him as an expert.

Cindy was less sure. She had been against not making reservations to begin with, saying that it was just plain reckless. "If he's not lying and we wait too long, we might be sleeping in an alley."

"Come on, that's exactly what they want you to think. They get you right off the train station. They scare you. Don't be a sap," Pea said as he picked up his backpack. "Let's go."

"Hold on," I said, stopping Pea. Even though it was my idea, hoping for the best, ran contrary to my nature. "Why don't we just make reservations, then if we find something better, just not show up?"

Cindy agreed, and Pea raising his eyebrows said, "If it'll make you feel better."

The young man was flipping his puka-shell necklace up and down with his thumb when we returned.

"All right," he said. "Twelve dollars a piece." This distorted things. "Yeah man, you gotta pay up front."

"Yeah, right," Pea said with a condescending laugh. He turned away, leaving Cindy and I behind.

The young man called after him, "We have to collect up front or else people would make reservations and never show up."

"Where else would they go?" Pea yelled. "I didn't think there were any rooms in all of Venice."

We apologized to the young man, who seemed unconcerned by the whole transaction. He reminded us that he stopped taking reservations at five. We hurried off to catch Pea, who wouldn't stop walking.

"You better be right," Cindy warned. "That's all I can say. You had just better be right."

"Do I look worried?" Pea quipped.

We spent the next three hours being told by every hotel and hostel that there were no rooms to be had in all of Venice.

"It looks like I might have been wrong," Pea said.

Not knowing where I was going to sleep that night made me nervous.

The campgrounds guy was sprawled out on the steps eating beans out of a can when we returned. "It's too late," he told us. "I stop taking reservations at five." It was ten minutes past.

All of a sudden this was serious. "Are the campgrounds booked up?" I asked.

"I really don't know." Or care, by the tone of his voice. "I just take reservations until five then somebody comes and takes them back to the site." He laid his can down and pulled an orange out of his brown paper sack.

Was it possible that there was no place to stay in all of Venice? My mouth went dry. Panic made a triumphant return to my stomach. "What are we gonna do?" I asked the others.

Cindy gave Pea a stern look. Pea scratched his thighs briefly. "Hey, I'm really sorry if I was rude to you earlier today. It's just that we are constantly having people try to scam us, and well, I'm sorry."

"That's okay, dude," he said. "People always think I'm trying to trick them, but I'm not."

"I know," Pea said.

"There aren't any hotel vacancies in Venice right now," he said.

"Believe me, we know."

The young man ate a piece of orange. We stared at him helplessly for a few moments, then asked, "How will we be able to know if there's any cabins left?"

"You just have to go out there." He handed us a brochure. The details were on the back.

"They won't be sold out, right?" Pea asked.

The guy just shrugged his shoulders.

Pea winced as he looked at Cindy. "You better pray," she said.

An older Italian lady sat at the campground's office listening to a portable radio plugged into the wall. "You have tent?" she asked us.

"No, we need a, uh, cabin there." I told her. My index finger was twirled in a circle to encompass the three of us, "Three beds."

She studied a piece of paper on a clipboard. It had sixteen large circles on it, four rows of four, each with an identifying number beneath it. The circles had four dashes inside them, lined up in two rows of two. This was pre-printed. Most of the dashes then had an X marked on them in red pen.

"No three beds together. Some cabin have two. Some cabin have one. No cabin have three."

We agreed to a two and a one. She dangled two small keys. Pointing at me, she asked Cindy, "You share with him?"

Pea said, "No. She shares with me."

The old woman winked at Pea and laughed. "You have to keep eye on the young." Pea bristled but held his tongue.

It turns out "cabin" was a euphemism for "shit box." These plastic huts were round, white chunks of fiberglass. Glorified port-a-pots. "These look like fricking igloos," Pea said.

"Fugging," I said, turning the key in my door.

"I'm going to kill you."

Each igloo had two sets of bunk beds and a small bathroom. There was a light, I assumed, but I couldn't find the switch. Pea held the door open, utilizing the outside utility pole. The one set of bunk beds already had backpacks on them, but I had my choice of the other. I tossed my gear on the bottom, "Let's go eat."

Dinner at the campsite was a little tense. We only had one day allotted to Venice and it was squandered. If Pea hadn't been so stubborn we could have made reservations and not had to return so early. If I hadn't insisted on "no advanced planning," the predicament would have never presented itself.

At half past eight I retired to my shit box in a sour mood. I stared at the other backpacks in the cabin. Stuck with strangers. Great. What if it was two big, smelly Germans who stunk up the place? Or what if it was a couple obnoxious Australian rugby players who came in drunk and pissed on me? Damn you Pea.

Eventually the door opened and my bunkmates were revealed. The lighting was too poor for a clear look, but their voices were sweet and girly. "I hope we weren't being too loud, we're a little drunk." My mood brightened.

Dear Penthouse. I always thought the things I read in your letters were made up, until I stayed at a campground in Venice.

We spoke as they prepared for bed. They were sisters from Windsor. They had saved up their tip money as cocktail waitresses to take this trip. In the darkness, the girls wiggled out of their shorts and jumped into bed.

*We hadn't been alone for two minutes and the sexy sisters
from Canada were removing their clothes and getting into bed.*

"Have you been in Europe long?" I asked.

"A couple of weeks," the girl on the top bunk said.

"You been having fun?"

"Yeah, it's been pretty fun," she said.

*Clearly sparks were flying. Was it possible these ladies were
thinking the same thing I was?*

"I'm just getting started. I'm going to Rome next," I told them.

"That's where we're going next," said the girl on the top bunk.

*Yes! Now it was her sister's turn. I sensed she was equally
interested.*

"I'm beat. Do you mind if we not talk tonight?"

"No, I agree," said the other. "No offense, sir."

Fug!

The harsh smell of marijuana woke me the next morning. The door
was cracked open filling the igloo with daylight and presenting me with a
decent look at the girls. They were nice looking in a bleached blonde,
eighties hair-band groupie kind of way. The one on the top bunk was
inhaling marijuana through a pipe. Her ears sported six earrings each and
both eyebrows were pierced. She passed the bowl to her sister.

The smoke filling our cabin caused me to cough.

"Oh, hey," the other sister said, a long bare leg outside the covers.
"Smoke?"

I looked at my watch. It was 8:10. Pea and Cindy wanted to leave at
8:45. "Not right now, thanks."

With nothing on but my underwear, I wiggled out of my sleep sack,
stood up and quickly wrapped a towel around my waist.

"You didn't look that tall in bed," one girl said.

"I'm shorter when I'm lying down." I pulled my toiletries and tennis
shoes out of the backpack lying underneath the bed.

"How tall are you?" asked the other.

"Six four."

"Wow."

When I returned from the shower the girls were eating chocolate chip
granola bars. No one spoke as my underwear was slipped on beneath

the towel. After my shirt and socks, the towel dropped to the floor and the shorts came up.

"You still going to Rome today?" they asked.

"That's the plan."

"You want to ride down with us?"

Maybe Venice wasn't a bust.

"Pea," I said outside his igloo at 8:50. "This is Sarah and Amanda." Sarah was the piercing freak, chubby with a pretty face. Amanda was taller with big fake cans and tacky clothes. Her cutoff jean shorts couldn't have been shorter and still visible. "They're going to Rome with us. Ladies, this is Pea."

They laughed at his name.

"David will be fine," Pea replied, looking a little shell-shocked.

Cindy walked to the door. Her hair was wet. "This is Pea's wife, Cindy. Cindy this is-"

"I heard," she said.

Cindy needed five more minutes. The girls walked back to our cabin to have a smoke. They didn't specify what kind.

"Man, Vic," Pea said, after they were out of earshot. "Those girls are little rough, even for you."

"I don't know that my mom would approve, but we are an ocean away."

Pea sniffed the air. He stepped outside and shut the door behind him. "You reek of pot," Pea whispered. "Are you stoned?"

"No, I don't do that shit. It's from the girls. They were smoking in the cabin all morning."

"There is no way that those girls are traveling with us," Pea said. "Cindy would shit herself if she knew they did drugs. She's very religious. I'm not even allowed to drink one fucking beer. This is no good. You have to get rid of them."

I laughed. When Pea gets worked up he looks ridiculous. His eyes bulge. The veins in his neck pop out. His arms flop spastically. Funny stuff. "It'll be fine, Pea. I promise."

"It's going to ruin the trip," Pea said in a whispered yell.

"It ain't gonna ruin shit. I respect your predicament; I'll keep things under control, but come on, Pea, what would you do if you were me?"

"They're white trash," Pea said.

"No, they're just Canadian."

ROME
October 8

Pea and Cindy sat back in coach with our bags. The ladies and I sat three abreast in the smoking compartment. Every time the refreshment cart went by we purchased Heinekens. By our second beer I had my arms around both girls. By our fifth I had seen their tattoos.

Upon our return to coach, I tried to conceal my drunkenness from Pea. Sarah and Amanda seemed fine. My lack of heavy drinking the past few years had lowered my tolerance to begin with, and even in my wildest days I couldn't have held pace with Canadian barmaids. Cindy was researching her travel guide for lodging.

Amanda and Sarah already had reservations at a hostel. I suggested we check it out. Pea made a sour face.

Cindy patted his knee. "It's worth a try." She actually seemed the more tolerant of my situation.

At the Stazione terminal in Rome, I fell flat on my back. The weight of my backpack was too much for my drunken legs to handle. Like a turtle turned over on his shell, I couldn't get up. Amanda and Sarah howled with laughter.

"Thanks for keeping things under control," Pea said. The girls reached down and picked me up. The three of us walked arm and arm to the Lucky Duck hostel. Which to my great joy, and Pea's consternation, did have more beds available.

In my mind it was a done deal that we'd stay there, but Pea insisted we look it over first. We'd never seen a hostel before, but no one expected much in the way of comfort, and to that end, we weren't disappointed. The Lucky Duck had three large rooms filled with bunk beds. In total it could sleep about 36 bodies, with two toilets and two showers to accommodate everyone. It also had a small kitchenette area where one could keep food and cook. It was 15 dollars American per night.

After the tour, the heavy-set girl managing the place looked at Pea and said, "I should warn you though, most people who stay here are still in their twenties."

"I'm actually twenty-nine," Pea said.

"Don't worry. It's not a rule or anything," said the girl. "We're not going to card you." She thought Pea was insulting her intelligence.

"I'm not fricking lying," Pea said, his voice rising with anger. "I really am twenty-nine."

"Let it go, Grandpa," I said. "The lady just said it didn't matter." Fully aware of the irony, Pea seethed.

Not wanting to stir animosity, or ruin anyone's trip, the sisters and I agreed to part ways until that evening. An exact time wasn't set, but it would be no later than 11 p.m., when the Lucky Duck doors were locked to enforce its curfew.

Cindy dragged Pea and I through an exhausting walking tour of the Coliseum, the Roman Forum and Palatine Hill. Back at the hostel, the three of us discussed our day.

"You know what I found funny today?" I asked. "Remember at the Coliseum, when that tour guide pussy-footed around the comedy events?" Besides the gladiators and the beasts, there was a comedy part. It consisted of retarded people fighting a group of midgets.

Pea chuckled, catching my drift. "The part about us evolving, you mean?" The tour guide prefaced the comedy part by saying that it was considered funny back then, but hopefully the human race has evolved past that kind of behavior.

"Yeah, no way have we evolved past that," I said. "If they had a retarded person fighting midgets on pay-per-view, it would make more money than professional boxing."

"Who do you think would win?" Pea asked.

"Oh, the retard for sure," I said. "They're strong."

"But a group of midgets," argued Pea. "Think about it. They're smarter, they're quicker, they can come at a retard from all angles."

"Stop saying retard," Cindy scolded Pea.

"But retards have an amazing tolerance for pain," I reminded Pea. Cindy made a face. "Sooner or later, the midgets would have to get into a physical confrontation, then the retard would beat their collective asses."

After a lengthy discussion, Pea and I agreed if it were simply hand-to-hand, the retarded person would win, but if weapons were involved then we would put our money on the pack of midgets.

"You guys are sick," Cindy accused. "Just because you two haven't evolved doesn't mean the rest of us haven't."

"Come on. The world hasn't evolved at all," I stated. "You read the Bible. The most recent of that stuff is two thousand years old. The reason the Bible is still valid is because we haven't evolved. The stuff it said not to do then is the same stuff we do now."

Cindy was about to counter point me, but I nipped it in the bud.

"The only difference is the technology. We have computers and cars and cell phones. They had scrolls and horses and uh, umm," I struggled to come up with the third comparison. "You know, shit like that."

"Our technology has surpassed our humanity," Pea added.

"Einstein, nice," I said.

"What?" Pea asked.

"That was Einstein's quote, don't act like you coined it."

Cindy jumped back into the fray. "I'm just saying that no way we would have midgets fighting the mentally handicapped."

"I'm not saying we would. I'm just saying if they did, a lot of people would watch. Look at professional wrestling. Do you have any idea how popular that is right now?" I asked. "And you think we've evolved?"

"But that's pretending," she said. "The Romans fought to the death. Do you think we would let people fight to the death?"

"No, probably not." When you added the death part it was a lot less funny.

"Then we've evolved," she said. "Now I'm going to bed. We have a big day tomorrow." Pea followed suit.

The girls returned just moments before the lockout. They brought some beer back and we drank in the kitchen. An Asian-Australian guy asked the sisters if he could join us. At 1:30 we were warned, for what the night security kid said would be the last time, too keep the noise down. "I better get to bed anyhow," I told the girls. "Apparently, I have a big day tomorrow."

After using the bathroom, then going back to the kitchen to throw away the cans the girls had left strewn around, I fumbled in the dark, seeking my bed. In the blackness, I heard a feminine voice say, "Vic."

Another voice giggled.

"Yeah?" I whispered.

"What are you doing?" The voice asked, too drunk to whisper.

Someone shushed her.

I walked across the room until I located the voice. It was Amanda. She grabbed my hand and pulled me near to her on the top bunk. "Hey, you," she said, sort of loud. Another shush from the abyss. Amanda took her hand and blindly patted my face. I leaned in and brushed her hair with my hand. We kissed. Her mouth reeked of alcohol, nicotine, and Crest.

She was a bad kisser. Her tongue never moved. It was like kissing the thumb end of your own fist. I would have gone to bed that second if I hadn't felt two small hands from the bottom bunk fumbling with the button of my shorts. Within seconds I felt her tongue ring. My legs shook, and I engulfed Amanda's mouth to muffle my moan.

The door opened and the light from the hallway illuminated the room. "Damn," said the Australian quite loudly. Between the noise and the light he woke everyone in our dorm.

"Shut that door," I yelled.

He stepped in and the room quickly returned to darkness.

"Dog gone it, Vic," Pea yelled.

Terrified of being tossed out of the hostel, I stepped over my shorts and ran back to my bed.

You never know what's going to spark the fuse that sets off the explosion. Sometimes it's social injustice. Often it's a perceived insult. This time it was just a stupid little meaningless word. Cindy clenched her open hands slowly into fists, like a man does when he wants to hit you but knows he can't. Her upper body heaved with anger. "I cannot believe you said the 'F' word in the Sistine Chapel!" Day two in Rome was not off to a good start.

It really wasn't that big of a deal. A short, dumpy Brazilian man blatantly ignored the rules and took flash photos inside the chapel. Leaning into Pea, I whispered, "Is nothing fucking sacred?" Cindy overheard, angrily snapped her pudgy fingers and then stink-eyed me the whole way out.

"I whispered it," I said. "No one heard but you."

"You don't think God can hear a whisper?" she asked.

I laughed out loud. "You think that God is up in Heaven right now all pissed off because I said 'the F word' in the Vatican. I doubt he gives a rat's ass."

"First of all, I don't think it should be said period. But I haven't said anything to *you*." A poignant glance in Pea's direction. She breathed heavily, winded from hostility. "You sir, desecrated a holy place."

Again I laughed. It couldn't be helped. It was all just so ridiculous. "Desecrated? It's not like I took a shit or something."

"You might as well have! What you did was unforgivable. That place is sacred to people."

"I agree. That's why I was annoyed when that guy took the picture. Right, Pea?"

"Leave me out of this," Pea said. He knew he was in trouble by association, and he wasted no time distancing himself.

"If you think it was a holy place, then why did you use the 'F' word?"

"Not holy to me, per se, but I do respect how other people feel." My comment yielded a sarcastic "Ha!" from Cindy. "That's why I whispered it. Have you heard me whisper it any other time on this trip?"

"No, I certainly haven't," she said, crossing her arms. Pea nervously put an arm around her shoulder. I stood silently, hoping this would pass without further incident. "The Sistine Chapel is not holy to you?" Cindy said, throwing Pea's arm off her shoulder.

Here we go. I scratched my eyebrow and thought. Do I do this? Do I have this discussion with her? Ah, why not? "You ever seen pictures of prehistoric cave paintings? With the buffaloes and bears?"

She had. Her arms still folded, smug look on her face. Judgment was already passed; this was only to determine the sentencing.

"I think it's about the same as that."

"You don't feel like we're any more spiritual than primitive man?" she said, like I was ridiculous.

"What's the difference? They sat in a cave and prayed to paintings; you sit in a church. It's just like we said last night; the only thing that's changing is technology. If anything we're getting less spiritual. They saw God in nature. They prayed to the spirit of the animal to return to them so they could continue to feed the tribe. We say that God is everywhere, but we don't see Him in our food. We don't see God in our fellow man.

We see Him on a ceiling touching fingers with some dude."

"So what do you think God is?" she asked.

"The truth is I don't know any more than those people did. But whatever it is, I think it's inside us. He's not a painting or a stained glass window, that's for sure."

Cindy exhaled an angry breath, the smug look wiped clean. "Let's get out of here."

"I thought you wanted to see St. Peter's Basilica," Pea said.

"Not now. The whole place is tainted."

"They're a *reflection* of God, if that makes you feel better."

Cindy stormed off. "Don't be like that," I called out.

Pea poked me in the chest with his finger. "You're ruining the trip."

I've got to stop discussing religion with people.

The rest of my day was spent alone.

It was over with Pea, just like it was over with Wally. I knew that, and couldn't care less. *I'm* ruining the trip for them. *They're* ruining the trip for me. Maybe this was supposed to happen. Dump the job. Dump the girlfriend. Dump the past. It's not like any of them missed me anyhow. A new rep took my territory. Lauren had a boyfriend. Pea and Wally had their wives.

Stop looking back. Start looking forward. Sarah and Amanda would be more than happy to have my company. And they'd be a hell of a lot more fun...if they ever showed back up. I sat in the hostel kitchen until 11:00 p.m. The girls never returned.

The next morning, they came staggering in exhausted. They had missed curfew by ten "measly little minutes" and were locked out. Most of their day would be spent sleeping. Pea must have overheard Amanda and Sarah's tale of woe. His first words to me since the Vatican, was the warm invitation of "Are you coming with us or not?" I accepted.

They say you can't see all of Rome in a few days. Cindy was out to prove them wrong, or kill me trying. Maybe she was punishing Pea for inviting me along. Either way, we started the day by climbing the Spanish steps and then never stopped. We never took the metro or a taxi. We never sat down, not even to eat. Little Romulus just kept us marching.

No *Piazza* overlooked. No fountain not photographed. *Piazza Mattei* for the Fountain of the Tortoises, *Piazza della Repubblica* for the Fountain of the Water Nymphs, *Piazza Barbenini* for the Fountain of the Triton, *Piazza Navona* for the Fountain of the Four Rivers. I never had to pee so much in my entire life.

By the time we arrived at the *Fontana di Trevi* early that evening, I was miserable. My feet hurt, my back was sweaty, and I had spent the afternoon being openly loathed. "You guys do what you want, but I'm not moving for a while." I plopped down on the steps.

Pea looked toward Cindy. "I guess we can rest," she said, sitting down, but not too close.

"Let's walk to a McDonald's and rest there," Pea suggested.

"Yeah, right," Cindy said. "We're sitting in front of the most beautiful fountain in the world and you want us to move to a McDonald's?"

"Fine, wait here. I'm going to get an apple pie." Pea devoured three a day, minimum. He devoured them like most tourists went after *gelatos*.

"You know what? Maybe I'll try one." Cindy said.

"Get me one too, Pea."

"Indeed," he grumbled.

As per our custom, when left alone together, Cindy and I waited in silence. A few yards in front of us, a little Italian boy wearing short pants squatted down to feed the pigeons. They fearlessly approached him. The boy sprang up and flapped his arms, scattering the birds. Cindy ducked as they flapped past our heads. The boy immediately squatted back down and repeated the scene over and over. Eventually, the pigeons wouldn't return. He sat crouching, with his hand out, alone. The little boy cried.

"He shouldn't have chased them away then," Cindy said.

"I guess he just couldn't help himself," I replied. "That's what little boys do."

She gave me a crooked half smile. I pretended not to notice. Cindy rubbed the stubble on her legs. She hadn't shaved them since we left Amsterdam. It isn't uncommon to see women in Europe a little shaggy, and you know, while in Rome and all that jazz, but still...ick. "Oh, I've been meaning to ask you, is Matilda cute?"

"Who's Matilda?"

A small grunt. "Wally and Stacy's little girl."

I hadn't known what they named it. Matter of fact, this is the first I'd heard what they had.

"That's the first thing I'm doing when we get back to Purdue," Cindy stated.

She'd probably see it before me.

"Don't you just love Stacy?" Cindy asked. This was clearly some sort of test. She hadn't spoken to me in a day and half, now she wants to have a conversation about Wally's wife. Probably hopes I'll say something mean, so she can report it back to her. Commiserate together about what an asshole I am.

"I really don't know her that well."

"I thought you guys all went to Purdue together," Cindy stated.

"We didn't really know each other, though." Although friends forever, she and Wally didn't start dating until after college, and by then I was basically out of the picture. I had an opportunity to get to know her years ago when Wally, Pea and I went to Mexico. But I met a girl from Argentina and kind of disengaged from the group.

"Well, she's great. I don't know what I would have done without her. When we first moved to Purdue it was terrible. I was homesick and David was so depressed about not farming, he hardly ever talked."

"Really? He was that upset?" Nobody ever told me. One minute he's farming, the next thing I know he's back at Purdue.

"It was the only time I ever saw him cry. Don't tell him I told you that," she ordered. Cindy looked down trying not to well up. "But anyhow," she said, forcing herself to be cheerful, "once we started hanging out with Wally and Stacy things got much better."

"Nice."

"You know what Stacy said once, and it's true?" Cindy smiled just thinking about whatever that delightful comment was. "She said that happiness comes in a lot of different ways. But if you insist on being happy only one way, you miss all your other chances. And she's right. When we were farming, David was always fighting with his dad and uncles because he wanted to implement the stuff he learned in college, and they refused to change. So half the time he was in a bad mood. If we were still farming we would have never gotten to see Europe. We would-"

"You'd have never gotten to know me," I interrupted. "I think that alone was worth having your life's dream destroyed for."

Cindy half-heartedly chuckled, then asked, "Why is that?"

"I was kidding."

"I know you were, but it's sort of true. I'm not saying this to offend you or anything, but I remember one time we were out with Wally and Stacy. The guys told this funny story about you buying some girl a big cookie back in college. I asked how come they didn't hang out with you anymore, and Stacy said because you hate the wives."

"Oh, that's not true." Hate's a strong word. 'Felt irritation toward' might be better. Or perhaps indifference.

"Then why do we feel that way?"

"I don't know. Low self-esteems?" I tried to joke, but she didn't laugh.

"You've gone out of your way to make me feel uncomfortable."

"I'm sorry about the Vatican. I really am." Not really, but sort of, I guess.

"That was just kind of the last straw. Drinking, cussing, womanizing. Married people don't like to be around that."

"I'm not married." This sounded angrier than was intended.

Cindy didn't bristle though. She no longer seemed angry with me. "The only reason I bring it up is because I know for a fact that both David and Wally miss you a lot."

That choked me up. Cindy didn't push. She let me sit quietly. It's strange how the mind works. When Cindy said that, I immediately thought of my college girlfriend. Maybe it was because Pea and Wally were with me when I met her. She was 18 at the time, and I fell in love immediately. Receiving the love back was tougher, and those guys helped me put it together. They were also with me when it fell apart a few years later. It was my first broken heart, and it felt like death. I prefer to think about us before all that happened.

Looking up, I saw Cindy rubbing her hairy legs again. "Did you know that I was engaged once?"

She nodded her head yes. "I just found out yesterday, actually. I found it strange that nobody ever brings it up."

"Some stuff you have to lock away." Like the ring. That engagement ring is in a drawer with my diploma and a few other keepsakes. I don't know why I never sold it. I wouldn't give it to anyone else. It just sits there in a box. Untouched.

"You sound like David," she said. "He never mentions the farm, ever."

"I should have been there for him when that happened."

She patted my knee. "You didn't know."

Exactly.

"Besides, I think it will work out better. David will be a professor teaching what he loves. We'll be able to afford a small farm of our own." She smiled hard. "Raise some kids and show cattle and be 4-H leaders." I envied Pea at that moment. If I were an irritable, little bald guy, I'd be screwed, but Pea had nothing to worry about. "God has a plan," she smiled.

Does He? Pea wasn't a farmer. I wasn't married. Was it destiny? Is life leading us toward an end? Or is it our decisions? If I had dated a different girl in college, I'd probably have two kids already. I could at the very least be engaged to Lauren now. Would I be happier, or would I be longing for my current freedom? You don't know that anymore than you know what God is. Our lives are just paintings on a ceiling. But I did envy Cindy for thinking it.

"Let's toss a coin into the fountain," Cindy said. The sun had set and the whole area was lit up. It was a beautiful scene. "One coin ensures you'll return. A second coin grants a wish." We walked near the water, and with our backs to the fountain, tossed our coins. Each of us wishing for something that eventually we would have to make happen for ourselves.

Pea returned holding three rectangle pie boxes. "This is what I love about Europe," he said. "McDonald's apple pies."

"You're so right, Pea," I mocked. "The history, the architecture, that's all crap."

"You know what I mean. Look at this." Pea slid his pie halfway out of the box. "This is the old school apple pie we can't get in the States."

Cindy was just young enough she didn't recognize the pie, and foolishly showing her age, almost took a big bite. Pea grabbed her wrist. "What?" she asked.

"They're a little hot on the inside," I told her.

"Yeah, a little hot, like lava," Pea added. "But they're so fricking good. I remember when McDonald's stopped selling this type and switched to that bullshit Dutch apple." Cindy gently rebuked him for the use of "bullshit." "I'm sorry," Pea stated, "but in this case, there's no other word to describe it. Those new pies are a travesty."

"I gotta go with Pea on this one," I said. "The old style pie was better. But it's obviously not McDonald's. They know. Every place else gets these," I said waving the box. "America's lawsuit crazy. That's why. If they had to pay a million dollars to every kid who scalded his mouth on one of these, they'd be out of business in a day."

"I think historians will identify the date these were discontinued in America as the moment the lawyers officially took over and effed everything up."

Pea's statement was a profound one, so we let it hang in the air for a while. Pea and I each nibbled off one end of our pies, to let the filling cool. It was tempting, oh so tempting to take a bite of this delicious pastry, but lessons learned in childhood stick with the man, and both of us knew better. We would have to be patient.

"Vic. Yo, Vic." I heard my name. Pea closed his eyes and shook his head. The Canadian girls waved me over. Sarah with a big smile on her face. Amanda with her butt cheeks hanging out of her shorts.

"We were just talking about you." Sarah said when I met them.

"Oh?"

"We've been thinking," Amanda said. "That curfew shit at the hostel sucks, aye. Maybe," long pause to build suspense, "the three of us," eye contact with Sarah, big smiles, "could get a hotel tonight. Stay out as late as we want drinking. Then we could get back to the room and have our privacy."

"What do you think?" Sarah asked, giggling.

I think I would love it. I think it would be incredible. But Pea has to return to Holland soon, and I think I'll miss him. And I think I miss Wally. And I think I've chased enough people away now, that soon, they won't be coming back. And I'll be in the same rut. Five years from now they'll have families and futures and what will I have to show for my life? A story about doing it with two skank sisters from Canada. And I don't think I'll be one step closer to anything new, but everything old will have completely slipped away.

"Well?" Amanda asked impatiently.

"You know what?" I said. "I don't think I do that kind of thing anymore."

The girls were stunned. I hurried back to my friends.

"What was that all about?" Pea asked.

"Ah…nothing. Let's eat our pies."

Pea took a big, lusty bite. He immediately opened his mouth with the filling still on his tongue. "Ahh," he yelled. "It burnt my fucking mouth."

"Fricking," I corrected.

THE LOO VRA
October 16

A scrawny little black guy wearing blue-tinted sunglasses took a seat beside me on the train to France. I gave him the standard two-finger piece sign greeting. He responded with the raised fist and a rhetorical "What's up?"

Across from us, a blonde sat leafing through a woman's magazine written in German. From a fashion perspective she had a perfect body. Her clothes fit exactly right. There was no place in her blue jeans, for example, where she had too much or too little flesh.

"You look familiar to me," the man said to her. "You ever been to Los Angeles?"

"No," she said, not looking up from the page.

"Hmm," the black guy scratched at the tuft of hair growing on his chin. "What about New York?"

"Yes."

"There we go. Did you ever go to any comedy clubs? I'm a standup comedian."

She shrugged and flipped the page. Complete indifference. Beautiful women must get tired of being hit on. Of course, ugly women must get tired of being ignored. We all got problems.

Watching him strike out with this girl really amused me, because I had done the same 15 minutes earlier. I went the other route. I asked her about herself. She was going to Paris for a print job. Model talk for catalogue. And if I didn't mind she needed her rest.

"Have you ever been to a comedy club?" he asked her.

Without answering or so much as even acknowledging him, she reached into a bag and put on headphones.

He turned to me. "Apparently, she not familiar with my work."

Pea and Cindy had returned to Holland. The Canadian girls were never heard from again. I had just spent three days alone in cold, rainy Switzerland, talking to no one. I was definitely up for some conversation at this point. "Are you really a comedian?"

"Actor-slash-comedian," he said proudly. "Out of L.A." His hair looked very Hollywood. A tight round afro and a strip of hair following his jaw line from ear to ear. "I was doing a USO gig. No big thing," he said, like it was a really big thing. His name was Skinny. No last name. Just Skinny.

"Do you have a day job?"

"I work part-time as a shoe salesman." He lowered his voice so the model couldn't hear. "I'm trying to develop a sitcom out of it."

"A sitcom set in a shoe store, huh?" I grinned. This guy was full of shit.

"There's a lot of funny things that happen. You at a mall so a lot of different types walk in and out all day. Men, women, moms with kids, married guys with their mistresses."

"Really?"

"All the time. Those are the best. Because the men are rich and the women are gorgeous...and insane. Something crazy always happen. Either a fight or a blowjob. One time, I'm on my knees trying shoes on this bitch in a mini-skirt. She has on no underwear. I'm staring right at her shaved coochie."

I was beginning to like this guy. Colorful, witty, obsessed with women. He reminded me of somebody.

"She tried on every pair of shoes her size. At the end, he buys her two pair and tips me a twenty. I hand it back to him, and say, 'Believe me bro, it was my pleasure.'" Skinny waited for me to stop laughing. "They laughed too," he said, "and then this rich old bastard gave me a fifty, which he insisted that I take." Skinny was very amused by his own story. He didn't laugh out loud. Instead he covered his mouth and leaned forward. He laughed more with his face.

"He paid you fifty dollars to stare at his girlfriend's snatch?"

"I think it was twenty for staring at her snatch and thirty for the funny ending when he tell his friends at the country club or whatnot."

"That's great," I said.

"I'm telling that story the first time I panel on the *Tonight Show*."

"Can you say 'snatch' on network television?" I asked.

Skinny covered his mouth and pointed at me, like "Good one."

"Excuse me," the model said. "But what kind of shoes did she buy?"

We looked at each other and lost it. She stared at us for a moment like we were idiots, then returned to her magazine. I had found my new travel partner. Skinny, the 26-year-old comedian-slash-actor-slash-shoe salesman.

Admission to the Louvre was 45 *francs*. An additional 30 would buy headphones for an audio tour. Skinny said we didn't need them. Skinny was wrong.

The first hour was brutal. I was suffering art overload and a headache. Alone, each painting was a masterpiece. Together they were overwhelming. They might as well have just been wallpaper on the way to the *Venus de Milo*.

We stopped in front of *Napoleon's Coronation*. There was a lot going on in that painting. The Pope was there, Josephine. It drove me nuts not to know more about it. "Man, we got to go back and get those head-phones."

Skinny shook his head. "Let's just look around. I don't want to learn too much."

"Why not?"

We were walking again. Breezing by the paintings like they were pan-handlers. "Cause when you ignorant, you either just like something or you don't. It's simple. The only thing I really know about is comedy, and that's basically ruined it for me. I can't watch ninety percent of the acts."

"But don't you enjoy the great ones now on a whole new level?"

"Trust me, there ain't that many great ones."

We passed a lady with the tall boots/long skirt thing going. She wore bold framed glasses, naughty librarian style. "Speaking of great ones," Skinny said.

A quick scan for a possible boyfriend came up negative. Skinny rubbed his hands together and gave me a wink. He approached the woman. "Excuse me. You look familiar. Have you ever been to Los Angeles?"

Over the past two days, he had "recognized" girls at the train station, on top of the Eiffel Tower, in the Catacombs, under the Arc de Triomphe, at Notre Dame, at the hostel. Basically everywhere. He recognized more women in Paris than I did at my high school ten-year.

"We met in Los Angeles?" Her accent was Australian.

Skinny removed his sunglasses. "Maybe, let me think."

"Do you think it was at the shoe store?" I asked him.

"No."

"Are you sure? Miss, did you buy any shoes while you were there?"

She squinted her left eye. "I don't believe so, no." Slow. Suspicious. *What scam are these dudes running on me?*

Skinny tried not to act rattled. "I got it." He snapped his fingers. "The Improv?" No. "Was it the Comedy Store?" Again no, but the hook had been set.

"You're a standup comedian?" she said. "How wonderful. Have you ever performed in Australia?"

"Not yet, but we been thinking about it. Haven't we Vic?" Skinny introduced me as his road manager, establishing himself as the alpha male.

"Maybe Australia would be the place for you," I said. "Americans are getting tired of fart jokes and Skinny here refuses to evolve."

She laughed.

"He's kidding," Skinny said.

"Would Australians find a man talking about his tiny penis amusing?"

"I think so," she said. She couldn't look at Skinny without laughing. Skinny put his sunglasses back on. For the first time all trip, he had nothing to say.

"Perfect," I said. "We'll see you down under."

Skinny didn't recognize another woman in the Louvre.

The *Mona Lisa* is the museum's showstopper. A large crowd gathered around her with cameras and video recorders. It baffled me.

"This is why we need the audio tour," I told Skinny. "To find out why the *Mona Lisa* is so much better than everything else."

"It's probably not," Skinny said. "I bet there's a hundred better paintings up in this bitch."

People scrambled around us for the best spot to photograph from. "There must be something special about it, or it wouldn't be so popular."

"People just be star fuckers, is all," Skinny said. "The *Mona Lisa* all famous and shit, so it must be good. Same thing in Hollywood. Once a comic get a sitcom his standup life is set. He can sell out any club in the

country, because everybody think he must be the best comedian. But it
has nothing to do with that. They either have a certain look that's right,
or more likely a good manager. They could suck as a standup, but people
don't care because they saw the famous brother from television. It makes
me sick."

"Yeah, because you're not famous."

"Shut up." he said.

I looked back at the *Mona Lisa*. "Still, it's pretty cool to actually see it
in person."

"Yeah," Skinny said sarcastically, "I came all the way to Paris to look
at an ugly white woman."

"If you want to look at ugly white women, you could have just gone
to Wal-Mart."

Skinny actually blurted a laugh before he could get his mouth covered. "That's good." He talked all Def Comedy Jam like. "Don't go to
Paris to see the *Mona Lisa*. That's just an ugly white woman. Load up you
car and go to Wal-Mart. Save a brother some money." He really growled
the last word so it sounded like Waaall-Mart. Then he just said "the
Louvre" over and over in different ways. "My girlfriend want me to go to
the Loooove," then "my old lady took me to the Loo Vra" and finally the
exaggerated, "I want to go to the Loooo Vra."

People were staring. To me, it was embarrassing, but Skinny fed off
of it. "The Loo vra. Man, what's funny about the Louvre?"

"Maybe you could act like you got it confused with the loo."

"The loo? What are you talkin' 'bout, dog?" Skinny often drifted in
and out of street slang and cadence. Especially when he was "on."

"The loo is what Europeans call the bathroom. It kind of sounds like
Louvre. You could tell people you wanted to take a piss and you ended
up in front of the *Mona Lisa*." I felt embarrassed by Skinny's blank stare.
"Or maybe not."

"No, that's pretty good." His wheels were turning. "My girlfriend
wants me to go to the Looove. I said, 'Why bitch? I don't need to shit.'"

I winced.

"No, huh?" He thought some more. "My girlfriend want me to go to
Paris, France. I said, 'What they got in Paris, France?' She said, 'The
Loooove. I want to see the Loooove.' I said, 'You dumb bitch. That's
just a French word for bathroom. We gonna go all the way to Paris,

France so you can take a shit?'"

The absurdity of someone actually telling that joke in a room full of strangers was the funny part to me.

Skinny softly snapped his fingers several times, thinking. "This is a good bit. How do I tie in the *Mona Lisa* part?"

"You have to explain what the Louvre is first." Skinny looked at me attentively. "Have her say 'Not the loo,' which you thought it was, but 'the Louvre, where they have the *Mona Lisa*.' Then say the thing about ugly white woman."

"Shit. You my new joke writer," Skinny said excitedly, then jumped back into character. "She said, 'You ignorant mother fucker. I didn't say loo. I said the Loo vra. You know with the *Mona Lisa* and shit.' I said, '*Mona Lisa*, that's just an ugly white woman. You want to see ugly white women? Get your ass in the Monte Carlo. We going to Waaall-mart!'" He jumped up and down.

"I think you got it," I said.

"No shit I got it. I'm buying your … I'll buy you a drink tonight." Skinny started to leave.

"Where you going?"

"I gotta find me some paper and a pen," he said happily. "I'm going to Waaall-mart!"

"*Deux* Heineken, *s'il vous plait.*"

The bar had a Rolling Stones theme. They only played Stones music. The walls were decorated with Stones albums, magazine covers, and other memorabilia. A tall, lean woman wearing no bra placed the beers before me.

"*Merci,*" I said.

Her nod seemed condescending. She didn't acknowledge my tip.

Returning to my table, I smiled at a group of middle-aged locals. No one smiled back. Skinny removed four empties from our space. This was round three.

"It feels strange to be a foreigner, doesn't it?" I said.

"You can tell you're white," he said.

"Why's that?"

"You got to come all the way to Europe to feel uncomfortable walking into a bar. A black man gets to feel that way at home." Skinny tapped my bottle with his, then took a drink. He looked around the room. "Actually, I'm more comfortable here than I would be in Wichita, Kansas."

"Are they racist in Wichita?" I asked.

"No, not really. I could have just as easily said Omaha or Toledo. It just at these places when you walk into a bar, everyone aware that a black man just entered. Sometimes it a suspicious look. Sometimes it people overcompensating by being too friendly. But you always feel something."

Skinny's comment reminded me of Denny and I grinned. "I have a friend who's going to change all of that."

"Really?" Skinny said, sensing that it was some sort of inside joke. "Is he a politician?"

"No, he's a fat guy who dances at minor league ball games," I said.

"Another Malcolm X type then."

"Yeah, only more militant."

Skinny smiled, but his eyes were somewhere else. He'd been looking past me the entire conversation. I turned just as the bartender looked our direction. Her right arm was crossed and her left hand held a cigarette. She half-heartedly gyrated to "Angie." Disinterest was very sexy on her. Skinny sighed. "I miss my girlfriend."

"That's funny. You didn't mention having a girlfriend when you were 'recognizing' women all over the city."

"My ex. Dumb bitch dumped me."

"Ahh," I said, voice full of sarcasm. "That is sad. When you finally find that one special dumb bitch, it really hurts when you lose them."

"Mock my pain if you must. But the truth is, that's why I'm still in Europe. Trying to forget about her."

"Come on. A rising young comedian like yourself, you must have a girlfriend in every town."

"I'm not a rock star. I won't be getting that kind of action until I'm famous."

"How'd you meet this girl then?" I asked.

"Comedy club in Louisville," he grinned. "I do meet some. Actually, I haven't met a girl outside of comedy in years."

"What about the shoe store action?"

Skinny flashed an evil look.

I chuckled. "What happened with her?"

"She like the *idea* of having me more than actually having me," Skinny said. "Ain't that some cold shit. The truth is, she just stopped believing in the dream. When they first see you on stage, everybody laughing, they think you a star. But the next day, you just some guy who ain't never around and makes no money. They want all the glamour but none of the work. But I'll tell you what. She was good for me," Skinny continued. "Because I'm even more motivated to make it. Just so I can laugh in her face when I blow up."

We tapped our beer bottles together again and drank to spite, life's great motivator. We tapped our feet to "Under my Thumb", while watching the pretty bartender look depressed. "She reminds me of a girl I was seeing this summer." Even though she was ten years older, and much skinnier, and three inches taller, and...actually, with the exception of dark hair, she was nothing like Ashley.

"What happened with yours?" he asked.

"There's not much to say, really. She was just a little too young for me, is all."

"How old was she?"

"Eighteen," I said.

Skinny made an ornery smile. "How old are you?"

"I just turned thirty."

Skinny covered his mouth with both hands. "God damn, nigger," he said. "I thought we were about to have a serious conversation on our last night here together, and you let loose with that."

The blood came rushing to my face. I decided right then and there to never mention her to anyone again.

"When you were her age, she was like what, five?"

"Six," I said.

He stomped his foot and clapped his hands. "Like that's better. She's wasn't in kindergarten, she was in first grade. If they can spell they name, they fair game."

"She wasn't six when I dated her. She was a legal adult."

Skinny had both hands over his mouth and rocked back and forth on his seat. He was loving it. Finally he composed himself enough to say, "I'm gonna miss you, brother."

"Why don't you come with me to London? It'll be great."

"Sorry, baby, you back on you own. I got to get home to Hollywood.

I ain't getting no sitcom over here."

"You have no doubt you'll make it, do you?"

"If I don't, I end up an old broke guy with no family and no marketable job skills," he said. "You start thinking about that shit, you go crazy."

Boy, did I know that. A lot of things that can make you crazy if you think about them too much. Her loving you, her leaving you, growing old, dying young, hating your life, changing your life. The list is endless and exhausting. Total waste of time.

The next day, I would be going to London by myself and it didn't worry me a bit. They speak English, I had a hotel reservation, and things would be fine. Traveling alone really isn't a big deal once you get used to it. And hell, you always wind up meeting somebody.

"Let me buy us another round, Skinny my friend."

"I got it." Skinny checked his hair in the reflection of a picture frame.

"You got the first two," I said.

"Call it even for the Louvre joke." I tried to argue, but Skinny was determined to buy this round, and for the five seconds it took him to get to the bar I thought he was being generous. "*Excusez-moi*," he said to the women bartender. "You look familiar to me. Have you ever been to Los Angeles?"

SHOE SHINE
December 1

A bald head peered over a *Journal Gazette* newspaper. "Young man," it said to me, "your shoes are in desperate need of a shining."

Without breaking stride, I looked down at my Doc Martens, scuffed, faded and worn out. Too many hours spent inches from a hot motorcycle engine, being dragged along the pavement at stop signs. "I believe these babies are beyond repair, but thanks."

The arrival board indicated that Flight 304 from Chicago, landing at the Fort Wayne International airport at 6:30 p.m., was delayed ten minutes.

"What you mean, beyond repair?" The short, round man called back at me. After folding the newspaper, he slowly crawled down from his elevated chair at the shoeshine station. "They got holes in 'em?"

"No, they don't have any holes. But they're pretty beat up. I just figured I'd get a new pair."

"What?" he exclaimed. "Why you want to go and waste your money like that? Get up on that chair and let me take care of you." He lifted his belly to tighten his belt.

"My friend's going to land in a few minutes," I told him.

"Plenty of time." He placed the silver shoe stands in front of the chair. "Besides, you can see everything you need to from here. Arrivals come through there." He pointed to the gate near the metal detectors. "And baggage claim is right over yonder," he said, pointing to his right.

I looked down at my boots. They really were beat up. I didn't want to waste five dollars. "I don't know."

He opened a tin of black shoe polish. "I'll tell ya' what then. You let me shine them free of charge. If you ain't pleased, you ain't out nothing.

If you is pleased, you can tip me."

I climbed up the step and sat down, placing my feet on the shoe stands. The old man wasted no time. He rolled my jeans up away from the leather and scrubbed my boots with a soapy brush.

"I been shining nearly my whole life. I ain't seen a pair of shoes yet, I couldn't fix up. You was gonna throw these out. That's why everything is made cheap now. Buy one pair of good shoes and take care of 'em. I've had my shoes for thirty-aught years. Been resoled more times than I care to remember. Comfortable. You young people spend your whole life breaking in new shoes. No wonder y'all so agitated."

He wrapped a rag around the first two fingers of his right hand and dipped them into the shoe polish, then applied it to my boots. This personal service made me feel guilty for some reason, so to avoid watching him, my eyes darted around. At least 80 pictures hung on the flimsy red backdrop behind the stand. Semi-famous personalities ranging from a Polaroid of a former mayor, to a headshot of Bobby Knight. "Whose the best person you ever shined the shoes of?"

"You mean most famous or most enjoyable?" he asked with a giggle. He was working the polish into my boots with a brush.

"Most famous," I told him.

"You ready for this?" He actually stopped brushing for a moment and looked me in the eye. "In 1973, right here in this very airport, I shined John Wayne's cowboy boots. Not just anybody can say that."

He sat down the brush and grabbed a rag. He whipped it in the air once. "Yes sir, this is the best job I ever knowed." He grabbed the rag with both hands and buffed. To each their own, I thought.

"Grandma," I heard a little voice yell. Two small children broke from a very frazzled mother to run into the arms of their waiting grandparents. They lead a group of passengers arriving through the gates that separated ticketed passengers from the general public. It was 6:44. This had to be the plane, but yet I didn't see anyone I recognized. Several people in suits talking on cell phones. An elderly couple being driven in a cart. Two young men carrying guitar cases. A middle-aged woman in sweat pants with a travel pillow still around her neck.

Just as the possibility of my friend missing his plane entered my mind, a scrawny black guy wearing blue-tinted sunglasses turned the corner. Skinny was chatting up a thick young lady with pigtails. Whatever he was saying seemed to be working because she was laughing. I waved both hands above my head to get his attention. He acknowledged my presence with a wave and pointed to the baggage claim.

Excited to greet Skinny, I looked toward my feet to see how much longer it would be. The boots were shined and the stitches were being traced with a yellow crayon. I couldn't believe my eyes. "Holy cow! They look brand new!"

The man gave me a proud smile and unrolled my jeans. "Kind of brightens you're outlook on life, wouldn't you say?" The man laughed after he said that, but it was true. For some strange reason it was exhilarating.

After stepping off the platform, I bounced up and down on my toes. I couldn't stop looking at my feet. "This is great." I pulled my wallet out of my back pocket and tipped the man a ten. He dug into his pocket for a five. "Just keep it," I said.

He insisted. "Five's enough. Nuttin' gives me greater pleasure than taking an old ratty pair of shoes and given 'em new life." He pulled out the silver shoe stands and placed them beneath his chair. "Now you go have a nice day." The old man then slowly climbed back up to his chair and resumed reading his newspaper.

Skinny barely acknowledged me when I approached him at the baggage claim carousal. He was a man doing well with a woman. Finally, at a lull in their conversation, I was introduced. "Vic, this is Patti. Patti sat beside me on the plane."

"Oh, lucky you," I said, ambiguous to whom it was addressed.

"Patti is going to come see me at the comedy club this weekend."

"I'm going to try," she said. She had a great set of teeth, white and perfect.

"You better do more than try," Skinny said. "I'll get you in for free. And I'll buy your drinks."

"Are you sure?" she said, clearly enjoying the attention.

"Absolutely," he said. "Don't worry about it. I'm in show business."

The alarm sounded three times to trumpet the arrival of the luggage. The first was a large, green suitcase with duct tape keeping it closed. Then two golf bags, followed by a big, horizontal suitcase with a handle on top and wheels on the bottom. A short, Italian-looking guy snuck up behind Patti and poked her in the back. Squealing, Patti turned and jumped into his arms. He lifted her into the air as they embraced. Skinny stared at them, bewildered.

When Patti's tennis shoes touched back down she turned to us. "Chad, this is Skinny. He's a comedian from Los Angeles."

The young man said "Hey." Skinny didn't respond.

"He's going to be at the comedy club this weekend. He can get us in for free."

"Really?" Chad asked, more suspicious than excited.

"Don't worry about it," I said. "He's in show business."

Patti hugged Chad again. "Oh, I've missed you so much." She kissed him with so much enthusiasm that he pulled away out of embarrassment. Patti put both hands on his blushing face and kissed him again.

I laughed quietly in Skinny's face. He looked away, refusing to comment. Chad pulled Patti's suitcase off the conveyer. "It was nice meeting you, and we'll see you at the show, hopefully," Patti said. Chad slapped her rear.

After they were out of sight, Skinny wanted to leave. "What about your bag?" I asked.

He stroked the overstuffed blue duffle bag hanging over his shoulder. "Carry-on."

I laughed again, "Oh, Skinny."

"That bitch never once mentioned she had a boyfriend."

COMEDY CLUB
December 1

There was a line stretching out the door to buy tickets when we pulled into the parking lot of the comedy club. "This is a good sign," Skinny said, unable to contain his excitement. "Thanks again for driving me around this weekend." The club only paid him $350 for the Friday through Sunday shows. His airline ticket was $260. If he had to rent a car, he would have lost money on the gig.

I was delighted to chauffeur him around and a little flattered. "You didn't take a low-paying gig, just to see me, did you?"

It was almost insulting how quickly Skinny dismissed that thought. "It's all about the tape," he said. On Sunday nights a local talk show was recorded from the comedy club. Performing on that would give him a professional quality tape to send to bookers of other clubs. "But it's nice to see you, too," he added, sensing my hurt feelings.

Skinny would be the feature, or middle act in a three-comic show. The other two were already in the greenroom when we arrived. The emcee, a young guy with round granny glasses, looked into the mirror and made faces. He wore a blue blazer over a black T-shirt. "Is-is-is one of you, one of you, S-s-kinny?" he stuttered.

"I am," Skinny said.

"What would you, uh, uh, what do you want me to s-say about you?" the emcee asked.

"BET. Opened for Drew Carey. From Los Angeles. Skinny."

"I b-better write this down," the emcee patted his jacket for a pen, came up empty, and left the room.

The headliner, a 40-something white guy wearing cowboy boots with chrome tips, looked up from tuning his guitar. "You sell anything?"

"Nah," Skinny answered. "You?"

"CD," he said, not looking up from his guitar.

I recognized his voice from the morning radio show I listened to. Or more accurately, used to listen to, when I had my job. "Does your CD have 'Sittin' Down to Pee' on it?"

"It's a greatest hits," he said. I assumed that meant yes.

The emcee returned to the greenroom, which was actually painted blue, carrying a napkin and black sharpie. "Now it was BET, Showtime, and uh, wha wha what?"

"BET. Opened for Drew Carey. From Los Angeles, Skinny."

"Right, right." The emcee's hands shook so much he could barely write. "And, uh, um for you Randy?"

"Just Randy Rogers. Ticket price is $25. They know my work." He was awfully arrogant for a man whose breakout song, "Benedict Penis," dealt with his own impotence with a hooker.

A tall, skinny man with white hair pulled back into a ponytail entered the room. "You ready, Mike? We're starting."

The emcee followed him out of the room. Within seconds, "The Curly Shuffle" played on the sound system and from an off stage microphone Mike was introduced to the sold-out house. Skinny and I watched from the back of the room.

"Hello, everybody, I'm your host and emcee, Mike Busboom." Silence. "What? You're not here to see me?" A small tittering. "I read a lot of biographies. Here's what I've learned. No matter how much you achieve or how successful you become, within fifty years of your death somebody is going to write a book that insinuates you're gay." No laughter, but at least he wasn't stuttering. "James Dean, Bob Hope, Liberace. I mean come on. Liberace. Is no one sacred?" No laughter. "I just finished reading Gandhi's autobiography. He gave up drinking, possessions and sex. He would have been a lot of fun to hang out with." You could feel the crowd getting restless. Someone yelled, "Next."

"God damn," Skinny said. "Gandhi jokes. This kid obviously has no idea who his audience is. This ain't PBS. This is a bar full of drunk people who came to hear a man sing songs about his ball sack."

Mike hung in there, though. "I feel sorry for his wife. She was probably like, hey, I don't mind the lack of sex. You're old, bald and ugly. But this poverty thing? Come on, you're famous now. It's time to cash in. Just one beer commercial and we're set."

Someone else yelled, "We want Randy." The audience broke into applause. Mike continued his bit. "Hi, I'm Gandhi. After a particularly successful hunger strike I like to celebrate with an icy cold Bud Light. After going several weeks without eating, my stomach is the size of a pea. That's why I like Bud Light. It has half the calories of regular beer."

The crowd talked among themselves. No one was listening. A red light flashed in the back of the room. Mike acknowledged it by shaking his head, then finished his bit. "Or Gandhi Chevrolet. Your trusted name in used cars is Gandhi Chevrolet. January is our big civil disobedience sale. Nobody pays sales tax in January at Gandhi Chevrolet." He placed the microphone back into the stand. "Thank you, that's all I'm doing tonight." The crowd erupted cruelly.

"We have an exciting show tonight. Randy Rogers is here." The room went ape shit. "But first, our feature comedian." The audience groaned.

Skinny said, "I am going to rip these mother fuckers up."

After fumbling around in his jacket pocket, Mike was forced to introduce Skinny sans napkin. "He does clubs and colleges all over the country. He's appeared on the Drew Carey show. From Los Angeles," the emcee froze.

"Skinny," Skinny yelled, taking the stage. He was full of energy and stage presence. He pulled the microphone out of the stand and stared down the audience. The room got quiet as they waited for him to speak. "Look at all the white people," Skinny yelled. The audience laughed. "I feel like I'm being auctioned off up here." Applause. "Laugh all you like. You people make me mad, I'll move into your neighborhood. Fuck up your property values." Within 30 seconds he owned them.

The emcee joined me in the back of the room. I tried to avoid eye contact. Skinny's style was less about material and more about attitude and energy. He bounced around on stage, mugged, did voices, whatever it took. He did five minutes on how black women talk at church that killed in front of 300 people who'd probably never been within ten miles of a black church.

"And white people, you gots to beat you kids." He pleaded with the audience. "Beat 'em. Beat 'em. Beat 'em. Go home tonight and beat 'em. Just say, 'I know what you did.' They won't argue. They'll just wonder how you found out. None of this time-out bidness." He assumed the standard black-comic lame-white-guy voice. "Brittany. You settle down or you're getting a time-out. I'm serious, Missy. I'm not effing around here. That's it. Time-out. We are in time-out mode now. You heard me, I want your cell phone on vibrate. You are in time-out." He paused for the audience's laughter to die down. "Time-out. Time-out when I was a kid was when my dad rested his arm between beatings. He beat me with my toys. The man beat me with a Hot Wheels track, people. A Hot Wheels track!"

Ten minutes later, Randy Rogers walked to the back of the room. "Why is he still on stage? Give him the light. Let's go." The red light came on. Skinny didn't acknowledge it. He was on a roll and just kept going. He impersonated Michael Jackson and Mike Tyson debating first-date etiquette.

"Come on Paul, get his ass off." The tall sound guy flipped the light on and off, until Skinny finally acknowledged it by holding up his index finger. "My old lady want me to go to Paris, France..." Skinny closed with the bit we wrote at the Louvre. The crowd loved it. My mouth was agape as I witnessed something I helped create get huge laughs.

Tapping Mike on the shoulder, I said, "I wrote that joke."

"It's good," he said. "What'd you think about my Gandhi bit?"

How dare he even mention his piece-of-shit Gandhi joke in the same breath as my Louvre bit. "I liked it."

Skinny closed. The audience cheered loudly. Mike ran to the stage. "Let's hear it one more time for Skinny." A jolt of energy and appreciation from the crowd. They were still clapping when he made it to where I stood.

"Not too bad, huh?" he said.

Before I could tell him that it was great, Randy Rogers got in his face. "Hey, this is my show. These people paid to see me. When you see the light, you get off stage, son. You go long again and your ass is history around here."

For 25 minutes Randy struggled. Instead of singing the songs the audience had paid to hear, he was performing standup...poorly. "I make love to my wife rodeo style. I jump on, piss her off, and try to hang on for eight seconds. She don't mind that, nearly as much as she hates being taunted by the clown afterwards. I told my wife to do it doggy-style once. She didn't get it. She licked my face and pissed on the carpet. I rubbed her nose in it. Made her so mad, I had to bring back the clown." The audience was polite, but they were about as excited hearing his jokes as a ten-year-old is reading the birthday card attached to the present.

Skinny enjoyed every second. "He can't follow me. These people paid to see him specifically, and he still can't follow me. Every week I bury the headliner. Every fucking week. You think a club will bump a brother up? No. They keep you down as long as they can. But they only hurting the show. A show should build. Keep getting funnier. But when they put me in the middle. The show peak in the middle. You know what I'm saying?"

Randy picked up his guitar and sang. "Before I met you I didn't need therapy. My credit cards weren't maxed, it didn't burn when I'd pee. And that makes me a horse's ass for loving you." The crowd went ballistic. "Horse's Ass" was Randy's newest song and had been receiving a great deal of radio play, even beyond the morning show.

The audience sang the chorus with him. "You're a lying, cheating, whore, but I couldn't love you more. You borrowed my Mercedes Benz to go do it with one of my friends. You were rude to my mom and dad, but you're the best lay I ever had. And that makes me a horse's ass for loving you."

Skinny's mood quickly darkened. "How hacky can a guy get? Whoever said sarcasm is the lowest form of wit, never saw this guy's act."

The last verse was sung *a cappella*. "If I'd have skipped you and done heroin instead, I'd be healthier now and money ahead." Randy strummed the guitar again, "And that makes me a horse's ass for loving you."

Skinny couldn't take it anymore. We moved to the lounge. "I'll get us some beers," Skinny said. "You grab some seats." I selected a dark corner booth so we wouldn't be bothered.

I glanced down at my shiny boots and smiled again. Who knows why it made me so happy, but it did. I thought about the old man who shined them. He said nothing gave him greater pleasure than taking an old ratty pair of shoes and giving them new life. New life. Perhaps it reminded him that it's the simple pleasures that make you happy. Maybe the activity put him in a compassionate mind-set. No matter how beaten down or scuffed up a person has become, with a little attention you can fix them up, give them new life. The act of shining shoes, suddenly stopped being a menial task in my mind and became a dignified spiritual exercise.

When Skinny returned with our beers, I asked him, "Do you sell a lot polish at the shoe store?"

Skinny quickly looked around to make sure no one heard me. "Don't mention that shit at the club," he said. "They need to think this is my only job." He hadn't sat down yet. "Let's move over there." Skinny wanted to sit near the women's restroom so he would be more easily spotted by the ladies.

"Why you asking about shoe polish?" he asked.

"I'd like to start shining shoes."

Skinny raised an eyebrow. "You know there's no money in shining shoes don't ya'?"

"It's not really about the money," I said.

"Oh, the pussy then," Skinny mocked. "Good luck meeting girls with polish all over your hands."

Two women exited the ladies room. "Oh my God," one of them drunkenly said to Skinny. "You were so funny."

"I like you better than this guy," the other one said.

"I get that a lot," he replied matter-of-factly.

Tall, lanky Paul had momentarily abandoned his station in the sound booth to get a drink. "Nice job, Skinny," he said. "What are you doing on the show?" Besides being the sound-booth guy, Paul also produced the Sunday night television program.

I was thrilled to hear Skinny say, "The Louvre bit." And even more thrilled to hear Paul say, "Yeah, I think that's your strongest stuff."

Skinny introduced me to Paul. "You want to come back to the taping?" Paul asked me.

"He my ride," Skinny said. "He'll be back every night."

"Great," Paul said. "It's not sold out yet. I'll comp you a table of ten if you can fill it." I thought I could.

"What about us?" The drunk women were still standing there. "We want to see a taping."

Skinny put his arms around both ladies. "Yeah, Paul, you got two tickets left for some of my fans?"

"I think we can do that," Paul said.

"Actually four," the one woman said. "Our husbands will want to come too."

The ladies went back into the showroom giggling. Paul left to make the reservations, and Skinny shook his head. "What's wrong with the women in this town?"

MY DESTINY
December 2

Dad sat on a dining room chair. His work boots rested on an old wooden milk carton I had brought in from the barn. I sat on my knees with my newly purchased shoeshine supplies spread out on a newspaper beside me.

"They look a lot better," Dad said. I had just finished buffing them with a rag.

"They look better," I agreed. "But they don't look new. Let me try again."

Since returning from Europe, life had been pretty lackluster. It was too cold to ride my motorcycle. I was sick of traveling. I hadn't met any new girls. Basically, my days were spent at coffee shops reading Taoism books. My nights were spent at home arguing with Dad over which television program to watch. Shining shoes would give my life the direction it needed.

"You got any shoes you want shined?" I asked my mom, who had been out in the barn, when she entered the kitchen. "I need the practice."

"Practice for what?" she asked.

"Vic's gonna be a shoeshine boy."

Mom laughed. She took off her coat and placed it on the back of a dining room chair. Feverishly, I buffed Dad's left boot, trying to get a shine. She took a long look at my supplies on the newspaper. "You're joking, right?"

"No." I said. "I think I might shine shoes for a while."

Mom stood over me silently as Dad and I discussed how to get the boots shinier. Maybe I needed more polish. Maybe I needed to buff faster. Maybe these boots just didn't get shiny.

"Fine," she said. "That sounds great."

"Yeah, I think so." Distracted. Buffing again.

"It's perfect," Mom added. "You'll have a job, and you can get your own place."

The buffing ceased. "I don't think I'll make that kind of money."

"You better get a second job, then."

"You let me live here when I had no job. Why do I have to move out if I shine shoes?"

"You said you quit your job because you wanted to find your destiny. Well, clearly, you found it. The high-paying sales job was only getting in the way of you shining people's shoes. Now move on with your life."

"I don't think shining shoes is my destiny."

"It's not?"

"Of course not. It's just a job."

"Oh, so you're ready to work now, huh?" Disgusted that I fell into her word trap, I remained silent. "Then you better shine a lot of shoes or find a job that pays you something. You have a college degree. You have sales experience. I'm not going to support you so you can be some crazy thirty-year-old shoeshine boy."

"You're thinking of this wrong. It's not really a job. It's a spiritual activity. Jesus washed people's feet. I'm going to shine shoes. Don't you get it?"

"Oh, I get it." The stony timbre of her gaze told me that *I* was the one who didn't. "Jesus didn't live with his parents. And neither will you."

"You're kicking me out?"

"Yes."

I looked up at Dad. "We'll give you until after the holidays to find a place." I tossed the rag aside. His shoeshine was officially over. "On some level, Vic," he said, "life is about struggling. Constantly trying to improve yourself. That's how you grow."

"If we let you keep living here, you'll never be forced to move on with your life," Mom added. Their speeches had the ring of rehearsal in them. "Five years, ten years will pass. You won't be able to get a job. You'll be alone. We're not kicking you out because we don't love you. We're kicking you out because we do. You've got to start living again."

Panic mode set in. This would destroy everything. I might as well not have quit my job or sold my house if I were going to go back to work within a year. I needed more time. "Maybe instead of moving out, I should just get some therapy or something."

"No, you're fine," Mom said. "You just need to go back to work."

"I'm not fine. What about my chemical imbalance?"

"Do shoeshine boys get health benefits?"

THE KOMETS
December 2

The usher escorted us through Memorial Coliseum, midway through the first period of the Komets-Indianapolis Ice hockey game. Upon viewing our seats, Skinny did a double take. "Tell me this shit ain't for real." But it was for real.

The line between regal and ridiculous was not a thin one in regards to the Fort Wayne Komets mascot - and our host for the afternoon - Fat Denny. He was seated on a throne - a plush, red velvet chair with gold fringe. His ass hung over both sides, where the armrests once were. His crown, a large purple hat, Catholic Cardinal-style, had a big "K" on it. This majestic regalia clashed with his tennis shoes, sweat pants, and over-sized hockey jersey.

In a somewhat misguided effort to make a positive first impression on Skinny, Denny waved his royal staff and proclaimed, "I bid thee welcome to the royal box of the United Hockey League's premier team."

Skinny pumped his fist. "Right on." In ordinary circumstances, I could have enjoyed Skinny's reaction to meeting Denny, but on this day, I was far too upset over my parents' betrayal.

"Rodney," Denny said, handing the usher an empty pizza box. "Please, bring us another pepperoni pizza and whatever these gentlemen are drinking."

I wanted a beer, but since no one was drinking, I ordered a Mountain Dew.

"This is some set-up you got here," Skinny said.

"Thank you. Most of the decorum was provided by me. Originally, they just had me sitting in the stands, but I feel this provides an atmosphere for a better show."

As Skinny and I unfolded our aluminum seats, the crowd rattled with excitement. On the ice in front of us, two players had dropped their gloves and were going at it. "Fight!" Skinny shouted.

The Indianapolis player was having the better of it. He hit the slightly larger Komet three times in the face before they fell to the ice and were eventually separated. The crowd cheered as the warriors were sent to their penalty boxes.

"Is it over?" Denny asked. His back was turned to the rink. As a peace-seeking Buddhist, it was wrong for him to enjoy violence. I tried to convince him that hockey fighting didn't count as real violence. He assured me that it all counted.

When the pizza arrived, we talked hockey. Which basically consisted of me saying, "The only sport I know much about is basketball." Skinny saying, "Don't ask me, I'm black. We don't do hockey." Denny explained every rule and nuance of a sport that nobody else in his company was interested in.

Denny and Skinny made quick work out of the pizza, but my stomach was too upset to eat. I had taken three little bites of my slice and put it down. "What's wrong?" Denny asked.

"My mom is kicking me out of the house."

"Why?"

"Because he wants to become a shoeshine boy," Skinny said, with a big, amused smile. He heard the story on the drive over.

"Did you explain it to her?" Denny asked. "How it's like Jesus washing the feet?" We had already discussed the matter in some detail over the phone.

"She thinks it's stupid," I said.

"It's not stupid. It's noble." Denny's mouth was full of pizza. "As a matter of fact, I've been thinking. Don't even charge for it. Or if you do receive money, give it to the homeless."

"You want my boy here to shine shoes for free?" Skinny said.

"It isn't money that enriches your soul; it's good deeds," Denny said, wiping his mouth with pizza crust.

"Right," I agreed. "And now my mom's ruined it. I have to find another place to live, which means bills, and rent, and having to get another job. This completely fucks up my spiritual journey."

"Not necessarily," Denny said. "This is a great test of your spiritual journey. Now you get to find out if you've learned anything, if you've evolved. Will you get a job and fall back into your old life? Or will you accept things as they come to you. Remember the teachings of Lao-tzu. Therefore the Master takes action by letting things take their course. He remains as calm at the end as at the beginning. He has nothing, thus has nothing to lose.' "

"This cat throwing some Obi-Wan shit at you," Skinny said.

"Obi-Wan lives in his mother's basement, so it's a little easier for him," I replied.

"It's no more easy or difficult. I just accept life as it comes to me. But I will say this. If you let your mom bully you out of shining shoes, you will regress to what you were."

"What was that?" Skinny asked.

"Rich and successful," I told him.

"You wouldn't want that," Skinny replied.

"Rich and unhappy is still unhappy," Denny said.

"Poor and unhappy is still unhappy too," Skinny added. "Only you got less shit."

"What am I going to do?" I asked.

"Stop thinking and end your problems," Denny stated.

"I've got to find a place to live, bitch," I snapped.

"Look at the birds," Denny said. "They don't plant seeds or gather a harvest-"

"That's the last thing I want to hear right now!" I looked down at my shiny, new-looking Doc Martens. "Piece of shit boots!"

"Fine," Denny said. "I have to get ready anyhow." There was less than one minute left in the first period. Denny stood and asked if we wanted another pizza. I angrily pointed at my uneaten piece. "Just asking," he said.

"That's the big advantage of hockey over baseball," Denny stated, as he tried to bend over and touch his toes. His ass was inches from Skinny's grimacing face. "Pizza instead of hotdogs. But they work me twice as hard, too. I have to dance two times instead of one. After the first and second periods."

"That is hard work," Skinny said, assuming Denny was joking.

Denny took offense to that. "It's not the dancing which is difficult," he said. "It's the constantly creating new routines. A lot of season-ticket holders come to most of the games. I want to give them something new to keep it fresh. Unlike say a comedian, who moves around from town to town doing the same jokes."

Skinny let the insult slide. "I see."

When the buzzer went off and the period ended, Denny opened a gate in front of our box. "Showtime." He stepped onto a stage that had been reinforced with steel beams. He was introduced to a large ovation. "Getting Jiggy Wid It" came on the sound system, and Denny did just that. The audience clapped along to the beat, and many danced in their seats.

"He may do different routines, but believe me it's the same joke," Skinny whispered.

"He does seem to have a lot of fans," I told him.

"His fans are the same people who think contestants on reality shows are celebrities." Skinny bit his lip, crossed his arms, and rocked back and forth in his chair. "Reality shows are shit. They're people who don't have the discipline to create an act, trying to be stars on a show where a producer doesn't have a desire to develop a script."

"You ever wanted to be on one of those reality shows?"

"No way," Skinny sneered. "I've applied to be on a few, just to see, or whatever, but I don't really give a shit." He stared at the ground, refusing to look at the fat, jiggling ass in front of us.

After his number, Denny stepped back into the box, flopped down on his throne and took a big gulp of bottled water. His torso heaved, and sweat trickled down his neck.

"Nice job," Skinny said.

"Thank you," Denny replied, taking a huge gasp of air. Denny's finger raised, signaling us to hold on. He took another drink of water, between pants for air.

"You all right?" I asked.

"I'll be fine." You could see stains spread on his hockey jersey as it absorbed the moisture from his body. He wiped his forehead with his wrist. "I'd like to discuss some show business matters with you Skinny."

"No problem," Skinny said.

Denny's body still heaved. "I wanted to wait until after my first set so you would view me as a peer when we had the discussion." Skinny's face quickly betrayed his thoughts about being considered the peer of a dancing fat man.

"What kind of comic are you?" Denny asked, still breathing heavily.

"I'm a funny one," Skinny responded.

"What kind of material do you do? Black people talk like this, white people talk like that, kind of thing?" Skinny actually had several jokes about how black people and white people differ.

"A little," Skinny reported.

"I don't like that. It's diffusive and cheap. Black people and white people are not different. They just try to be."

"That's not true," Skinny said. "We have a different way of talking. A different rhythm."

"I've been watching BET, and the speech is one of the things that I have listed as what's wrong with *Comic View*."

"You got a list?" Skinny asked. "A white man, who is not a comedian, got a list about what's wrong with black comics?"

"Yes," Denny said.

"Denny here considers himself a champion of black causes," I told Skinny.

"Not black causes. Human causes. Like the Dalai Lama said, 'My religion is kindness.' I want everyone to find their peace and dignity."

"Me too," Skinny said. "That's why I made a list of what bothers me about fat people."

"Please, be serious," Denny scolded. "You've seen some of those black stand-up shows on television. The grammar they use is horrendous."

"You see there Denny, that's how black folk talk when we together. You prefer us to talk white."

"First of all, I don't like that phrase, talking white," Denny said. "It's sour grapes. It's another excuse not to succeed."

"So you're saying to succeed we have to assimilate into the white man's world."

"The fact that you see it like that is the problem. It's not called talking white. It's called proper English. You don't hear Asians talking in stereotypes. They strive to better themselves."

"That's hilarious," I said. "That could be a bit. Militant Asians with broken English."

"Vic, please," Denny said.

"No," Skinny said. "Vic's right." Skinny returned to his *def jam* cadence. "How come only black people proud of speaking bad English. I ain't talking like no white man. You don't hear Asians doing that. 'Me uh na talky rike uh da rite man.'" He squinted his eyes and made buckteeth as he said it.

"That is very offensive," Denny said.

Skinny ignored him and continued riffing. "Black people say stuff like, 'He a good nigger.' You don't hear Asians saying, 'He most honorable chink.'" Skinny clapped his hands.

"That only proves my point," Denny argued as Skinny reached into his leather jacket. "You think it's funny because it's ridiculous. Asians try to better themselves. A militant Korean talking in broken English would be looked down upon in their culture for not educating himself. But I think some of these black comics are educated and talk like that on purpose."

"That's what the audience accepts," Skinny said. He pulled his comedy notepad out of his jacket and flipped to an empty page. "Black audiences hate a performer who thinks he's better than them. Some Uncle Tom will get ate up by those crowds."

"Are you hearing this Vic?" Denny shouted. "A middle-class educated black comedian, will speak poorly on purpose, to be accepted by a lesser-educated black community."

"So?" I said, feeling a tad uncomfortable. Skinny's act was none of Denny's business.

"So," Denny yelled. "This proves my essay to be true. That today black racism is holding back more blacks than white racism."

"Now, wait a minute," I said. "White audiences at the comedy club love that street shit too."

"That's even worse then. He just feeds the ignorance and the stereotypes. Skinny should strive to show a good example when he's on stage," Denny said.

Skinny didn't look up. His left leg bounced up and down as he wrote in his notepad.

"That's bullshit," I told Denny.

"Setting a good example is bullshit?" he mocked.

"If a white comic was pretending to be a hillbilly or a slacker drug addict, you wouldn't care. You'd say that's just a character. But Skinny can't do that? That's just as racist as anything else. He's not a politician. He has the right to perform any act he wants."

"If it's honest," Denny said. "But in most cases it isn't. These guys are like a civil rights leader who fans the flames of racism so he can profit from it."

"You don't know what you're talking about," I told him.

"Why, because I'm not black? It's racist to say I can't feel empathy for a human being of another color."

"I treat him like an individual. You treat him like a member of a race. That is the very definition of racism."

"You're nuts," Denny said.

"No, you are," I retorted. "Hey Skinny, who's the racist, me or Denny?" Skinny continued to write in the notepad. I shook his shoulder. "Have you been paying attention?" I asked.

"No. I missed most of it. I'm working out this new bit," Skinny said. He made a stereotypical Asian face again and said, "You my gook? Is uh you my gook?"

"I think we just found the racist," Denny said.

Skinny flapped his notebook in the air. "This is going to be a killer bit."

"Whose attitude do you think is more beneficial to the black cause?" I asked Skinny. "Mine, that a black person is an individual and free to say and act however he wants."

"Or mine," Denny interrupted. "That a black person should strive for intelligence and excellence in spite of a bitter peer group."

Skinny thought about it for a moment, then said. "You a big-ass dancing clown, and you a skinny-ass shoeshine boy. I believe the black cause will be fine without either of y'all."

I thought it was funny, but Denny did not. "This is why my essays have to be presented anonymously."

THE LAST LAUGH
December 3

Skinny paced back and forth in the comedy club lounge. "Maybe I should do the new bit." He had rushed us from the hockey game straight to the club, because he had to get made up for the show. But we'd been there a half-hour already and the make-up girl had yet to arrive. "It's funny right? Militant Asians with broken English. That's funny."

Denny snorted, but apparently as a peer, he knew not to say much before a show, leaving me to answer. "I think it's funny, but do you want to perform a brand new bit on television?"

"I know. I probably shouldn't. I wish I'd thought of it two days ago. I could have had it all worked out now." Skinny paced again, shaking his notebook in his hand. "But then again, this could be my signature piece, and I'll want it on tape."

Finally, Denny chimed in. "I've found when I'm performing something new that it's best not to think about it too much. A good artist lets his intuition lead him wherever it wants."

"That may work when you're trying to decide between the cabbage patch or the moonwalk, but comedy is a little more difficult," Skinny said.

"How much time do you get?" I asked.

"I'm not sure yet. I've got to get at least seven minutes or the tape is worthless. You watch the show," he said to me. "How much time do the comics do?"

"I don't know. I never really paid attention."

"Does it seem like seven? It's got to be seven. Damn, these stingy bastards don't give me seven..." More pacing.

His fears were soon put to rest. Paul, talking into his cell phone, approached our table. "Shit. Shit. Shit," he said after hanging up. "We lost one of our guests tonight. So were going to need you to do at least ten minutes. Do you have ten clean minutes?"

"Of course," said Skinny.

"Perfect. And you may be paneling with Alan afterwards. So we'll need you to write down some questions that lead into a funny story or bit."

"No problem," Skinny said, as he wrung his hands. The producer walked away.

"This is awesome," Skinny told me. "A ten-minute spot and panel. Man, this better than I ever dreamed." Skinny grabbed the garment bag with his change of clothes and ran toward the greenroom.

Denny and I sidled up to the bar to order drinks. The lounge was still empty, so we had the bartender's undivided attention. He was a pale man with sickly little arms and yellow teeth. I ordered a beer and Denny asked for an orange juice. The bartender took a long look at Denny. "Hey, aren't you that dancing guy?"

"Yes, I am." Denny swelled with pride, although, he was still dressed in his Komets attire, thus far from inconspicuous.

"I love you, man. You're the best part of the games."

"Why thank you," Denny said, then lowering his voice added, "I hear that quite a bit."

The bartender was quite disappointed to find out that Denny was only an audience member and not a guest for the evening's show. He still comped our drinks. I tipped him the cost of the beer, but to my consternation he stepped away before noticing.

"Do you think you could be on this show sometime?" I asked Denny, after we sat back down at a table.

"I'm sure I could. I just don't want to."

"Why not?" I asked.

"First of all, I'm more famous than I want to be already. That incident with the bartender is not uncommon. Secondly, being on television feeds the ego. You start to think you're better than other people, which leads to arrogance and puts you further away from enlightenment."

The pony-tailed producer returned, walking with purpose. "Excuse me," he said to Denny. "The bartender tells me we have a local celebrity in our midst this evening."

"Just a servant of the people," Denny said.

Paul spoke quickly, under duress. Showtime was in just over an hour. "We could really use a third guest for the show this evening. Would you be interested?"

Denny sheepishly grinned. "Oh, all right."

"Great," said the producer. "Why don't you join me in the green-room, and I'll introduce you to Alan."

As we entered the showroom, I asked Denny, "What about your enlightenment?"

"They needed help. That's all."

We followed the producer through the showroom, where Paul stopped just long enough to shout instructions at the camera crew setting up. Then through the hall, past the kitchen, and into the greenroom. There were several people in this small room. Skinny, now changed into black slacks and a purple sweater, sat on an old couch, writing out questions on a yellow index card. Randy Rogers tried unsuccessfully to tune a small television set.

Sitting on a bar stool, having his make-up applied, was the host of *Last Laugh*, Alan Dieter. Alan had done the weather for 20-some years on the local NBC affiliate, until "wacky" weather guys fell out of favor and he was replaced with a serious meteorologist seven years ago. To avoid a backlash from his fans, the station gave him a Sunday night talk show they assumed would fail within months. To their great surprise, it was a modest hit.

Paul put his hands on Denny's shoulders. "Alan, we've found a third guest." Skinny's jaw dropped. "This is Denny, he's the mascot for our local sports teams," Paul continued.

Alan looked Denny up and down once and smiled. "I recognize you. You dance, right?" Denny answered by raising his fists shoulder height and wiggled his upper torso. Alan laughed like a mule whinnies. "This will be great. We should've had you on a long time ago."

"Might I ask who cancelled?" Denny said.

"Babette, the circus poodle," the producer said.

"That surprises me. Babette is always very professional." Alan said. "I wish more of our guests acted like her."

"Do you mean the drinking out of the toilet or humping your leg?" Paul asked.

"Both," Alan said, with a goofy face. He was a cornball, but you couldn't help liking the guy. He just wanted everyone to have fun. You got the sense that even his odd-looking toupee was worn for laughs rather than vanity.

"Now if you don't mind, Denny and I have to coordinate his music with the band," Paul said. "We'll put him between the headliner and the feature." He turned to Skinny and added, "We're not going to need you to do panel. Sorry. You can still feel free to hump Alan's leg though."

Skinny wadded up the note card and sulked. I sat next to him, but didn't speak, fearing someone would kick me out of the room. A short, bony man with messy dark hair entered the room. He held three large pieces of cardboard with jokes written on them. "Here's the mono-logue."

Alan had him hold them up so he could read them. "The second one isn't funny," the make-up girl said. She was a petite little thing, but sassy, which made her unbelievably cute.

"Please," the writer shot back at her. "You cover up Alan's wrinkles, and let me write the jokes."

"First of all," Alan said. "I'm not wrinkly. And secondly, she's right. That joke's not funny."

"It's funny," the writer said, turning the card around to face him. "Listen. Recently in Allen County, undercover police busted several high school students for selling marijuana. Authorities first suspected drug use when the students voted to change the school song to 'Jammin.'" The writer laughed at his own joke. "That's funny."

"Sort of," Alan said. "It's one of those jokes that sound like they'd be funny but the audience never laughs at."

"Come on, Dude," the make-up girl added. "'Jammin'? That's a little obscure."

The writer glared at her. "I'm sorry. Perhaps you'd be more comfortable with a Brittany Spears reference."

She flipped him off.

"I think she's right, though," Alan said. "I don't get it."

The writer's voice raised two octaves. "'Jammin'. Bob Marley. 'I hope you like jammin'. I hope you like jammin'. I want to jam it with you'."

Alan looked confused. The make-up girl rolled her eyes. The writer shook his head.

Without thinking I said, "Puff the Magic Dragon."

No one laughed. It just sat there. Embarrassed, I tried to slouch deep into the sofa. Then Alan, without looking at me, said, "Better."

"Not better," argued the writer. "Just more obvious."

"More people laughing is better," Alan retorted.

I pressed my luck. "How's about, authorities first suspected drug use when the marching band stopped playing the fight song and started improvising long Grateful Dead numbers."

"Now that I like," said the make-up girl. The rest of the room agreed.

"You're pretty good," Alan said to me.

"He's great," Skinny chimed in.

Alan looked at his writer, then said, "I've been looking to add another writer. Would you be interested?"

"It doesn't pay much," the writer quickly added.

"He don't work anyhow," Skinny told them. They gave me a strange look.

"We'll see how much longer that lasts," I said meekly. "But I would love to help you guys write jokes."

"Welcome aboard," Alan said.

"How's about, authorities suspected drug use when the Home Ec teacher couldn't stop giggling on brownie day." Everyone laughed, but I think more at my enthusiasm than the joke.

Fifteen minutes before taping, Denny was still discussing his musical arrangement with the bandleader, whose patience seemed to be waning. "No, Denny, we don't need to rehearse. We know the song."

"But I'd like to hear you play it, so it sounds right to me. I'm the one with my face in the lights and my neck on the line."

Before the bandleader could counter, I broke in. "Hey Denny, they need you back in make-up."

"Thank God," said the bandleader. The rest of the band laughed.

Denny pointed his finger at each of them. "I'm not pleased with the lack of professionalism." They couldn't have cared less. The *Last Laugh* band was four aging factory workers, wearing *Last Laugh* T-shirts, being paid in beer.

As I pulled Denny away from the band, Kevin was being seated with his wife, Kylie and two other couples. Kevin had claimed seven of my ten tickets but had apparently only brought six. As the others sat down, Kevin took a few steps away and whispered into my ear, "Do you think your comic friend could mention my customers from stage?"

"It's a TV show," I said.

"I know. It'd be huge."

"He only came to get a good tape. He's not going to screw that up to help your sales," I said.

Kevin wrinkled his nose to show his displeasure. "I don't like your new friends."

As Kevin was about to sit down, I grabbed his arm. "Do you think that Nucroix would hire me back?"

Kevin's jaw tightened. He didn't need to speak to tell me the answer was no.

"Never mind," I said. "I was just curious is all."

Kevin's eyes focused behind me. "Oh, by the way, I have a surprise for you." He pointed to the double doors separating the showroom from the lounge.

In walked Lauren Reynolds...looking good. Looking damn good. She had a knack for choosing clothes that were appropriate for the situation, yet, attention grabbing. This evening she had a camel-colored turtleneck, a black wool skirt that was hemmed just below the knee, and tall, black leather boots.

Seeing her embarrassed me for some reason. "Hey, Lauren."

"Hello," she said, looking suspiciously at Kevin. She seemed equally surprised to see me.

"How've you been?" I asked her, when she and Kevin had taken their seats.

"Fantastic," she said. "And you?"

"Well, not fantastic," I said, standing over her.

"Lauren broke up with her boyfriend," Kevin said.

She blushed a little but didn't seem too torn up over it. "He was an idiot."

"You seem to attract them," I said.

The waitress finally turned up to take the table's drink orders. As Lauren ordered a vodka tonic, Kevin gave me the thumbs-up behind her back. Kylie elbowed him. "Turn around and leave them alone," she said.

I took a seat beside her. She smelled of vanilla. "You look fantastic by the way." She had let her hair grow out and added blonde highlights.

"Thanks," she said. "You look good, too." I gave her a "Yeah, right" kind of response. I was wearing an old pair of jeans and a brown fleece sweatshirt. "No. I mean it," she said. "The time off seems to be agreeing with you. You look really healthy and relaxed."

I shrugged. "I got your birthday card this summer. Thanks."

"I wondered if you received it. I thought maybe I'd hear from you."

"Yeah, I got it. It was nice."

"So are you happy with your decision?" she asked.

This made me a little uncomfortable. "I don't know. I miss you sometimes."

She playfully hit my arm. "Not to dump me, you jerk. To quit your job and travel."

"Sorry," I said, with an awkward chuckle. Lauren kept a dignified aura and waited for my answer. "I definitely don't regret doing it, I guess. But I'm not sure that it's changed my life or made me any happier."

"It changed your life a lot," she said. "You're now someone who has done it as opposed to being someone who wishes they could. I respect you for having the courage."

"Thanks." I had forgotten how delightful Lauren could be.

"What about you? How's the job?"

"Good. Really good. I'm up for another promotion."

The lights went down in the club and the band played. "I need to get backstage. But I would really love to talk with you afterward."

"Okay," she said.

"Promise you won't sneak out of here without having a drink with me?"

"I promise," she said.

I stood to leave, but felt it difficult to pull myself away from her. "Can I have a hug?"

She laughed but stood and gave me a long, firm hug. Kevin turned around and mouthed "Nice."

"Who was that you were talking too?" Skinny asked me when I joined him in the hallway leading to the greenroom. He'd been watching from behind the curtain.

"My old girlfriend," I said proudly, staring at her.

Skinny took another long look at Lauren. "She's eighteen? I take back everything I said."

"No. Different girlfriend."

"I bet you were sad when that went away."

"I broke up with her."

"Nigga, please."

The writer passed through the hallway carrying the cue cards. "Make sure you watch the monologue. It'll help you write for Alan. But I'll warn you right now," the writer quickly looked over his shoulder. "He always screws up the punch lines. Then he blames me for the jokes not being funny." The *Last Laugh* theme song ended, and the writer rushed to his place in front of the stage.

Skinny closed the curtain behind him and said, "I can't believe that fat friend of yours got my panel time." Although, he was actually far less upset than I expected. "Panel wouldn't help my tape anyway. I just need the seven minutes of stand-up."

Alan performed the monologue. The joke I helped write was butchered. He ignored the card and tried to combine two punch lines. It was delivered, "Authorities knew they had a problem when the marching band started improvising 'Puff the Magic Dragon'." The audience laughed, but not the big ovation I had hoped for.

Throughout the monologue, I watched Lauren. She laughed at my joke. We always did share a sense of humor. Sometimes, we would sit at a restaurant for hours and barely touch our meals because we were too busy talking and laughing.

After the third joke, Alan bantered with the band. This conversation was much funnier than the monologue. After a particularly entertaining question and answer about the bass guitarist's divorce, Alan told the audience about the comedians, leaving Denny as a surprise. Then he cut to commercial, with the band playing Rod Stewart's "Hot Legs."

Skinny and I ventured into the greenroom to find Denny arguing with the make-up girl about the correct shade of base for his skin. She, being spirited, didn't give an inch. "Hey, I don't tell you how to…" she stammered for a second trying to figure out exactly what his talent was, "eat," she finally decided. "You don't tell me how to do my job."

Not wanting to get involved with the unpleasantness, I returned to the hallway and stared at Lauren. She was up for another promotion. One of the great things about her is that she enjoyed working. You didn't feel the pressure to support her with a certain lifestyle. She could earn her own way…and then some.

The commercial break ended and Alan brought out Randy Rhodes, who debuted his new song "There are no gays at NASCAR." Skinny rolled his eyes, but the older comic killed. After the song, he sat down and did some of his stand-up material in response to Alan's prepared questions.

Alan broke for commercial promising the audience one of Randy's classic songs when they returned. The band played "Taking Care of Business" through the break.

Skinny said, "It's probably a blessing to have Denny dance between me and him. It will clear the bullshit out of the people's minds from this hack." Skinny figured time. The show, not counting commercial breaks, ran about 46 minutes. This is actually more time than most one-hour programs have, but *The Last Laugh* was a local show, so Alan did several promotional appearances each week that generated the bulk of the show's revenue. He was paid similar to that of a radio DJ.

The opening monologue and banter with the band lasted 11 minutes, 47 seconds. The headliner's segment lasted ten minutes, eight seconds. I know the time because Skinny was keeping it exactly, on a timer on his watch. "We have approximately twenty-four minutes left. Alan and the headliner will do another five minutes. Denny will dance about four minutes. That leaves fifteen minutes. Figure Alan screw with the band or whatever for five more minutes. That still give me ten."

After the commercial, Alan and the headliner paneled for another five minutes before the next song was sung. I'm not sure what they talked about because I was distracted by Skinny's non-stop muttering. "God damn. This mother fucker stole half those jokes. Let him sing his stupid-ass song and end it." All told, stupid-ass song and panel, that segment lasted another eight minutes. "No problem. We still have sixteen minutes. As long as the dancing bear keeps it under six, I'm fine." Skinny nervously air drummed to the band's rendition of "Walk This Way." "What does a song last usually, anyhow? Three, four minutes tops, right? Plenty of time, plenty of time."

The dancing bear, up next, turned the corner. He walked past me and took in the scene. He reached back with his right hand and grabbed his right ankle and pulled it to his ass. "All ready?" I asked him.

"Can't talk. I'm in the zone," he said, staring at the audience.

This cracked Skinny up. "He in the zone."

I was in sort of a zone myself. Lauren had said that she respected me for what I was doing. She didn't think I was a fool. She even hinted that it may have changed me for the better. No talk of grandkids and lake houses and embarrassment by my actions. She wasn't obsessed with how my journey affected her.

Soon the band wound up, and Alan said, "We're back. We now have a special surprise for you. How many of you have ever been to a Wizards or Komets game in Fort Wayne?" Most of the audience applauded. "For those of you who have, our next guest needs no introduction, but for the rest of you, please welcome Dancing Denny." The band broke into Rick James' "Super Freak." Denny told me later - after he'd gotten out of the zone - he picked the song for two reasons. One, it was really fun to dance to, and secondly, it sounded like "U Can't Touch This," by MC Hammer. He captured a wider demographic that way.

It seemed to work, because the audience went crazy for him. Denny worked it. He jumped and shook and shimmied. He did the running man, the cabbage patch, and something he called the Rerun. When he finished the audience jumped to their feet and gave him a standing ovation. Skinny exhaled a quiet, "Oh shit."

Lauren stood with a huge smile on her face. She looked really happy. I wanted to give her another hug. Then to Skinny's dismay, Kevin started a chant. "One more song! One more song!" The rest of the audience joined in almost immediately. "One more song! One more song!"

Denny standing alone in the middle of the stage, panting hard and sweating, took another bow. The audience demanded more. "One more song! One more song!" Denny turned to Alan and raised his palms. Alan responded by raising his right hand in the air with the index finger pointing to the sky. "One more song!" he chanted with the audience. The audience screamed and raised the volume on their chanting. "One more song! One more song!"

Skinny couldn't believe what he was seeing. "No. No! NO!!!" Skinny's lifestyle has to be understood to fully appreciate his anguish. Almost every week, he's in a different town. He'd given up having a home, close friends, and any chance of making a relationship work...for this, his dream. He needed a good tape, and to watch someone who had sacrificed nothing to steal his time was very painful. But that's show business.

"One more song! One more song!" the audience cheered. Denny proudly stood and accepted their love. He raised his hand to silence the crowd. He turned to the band, "Do you guys know 'Play that Funky Music'?" They nodded. "Hit it!" Denny said. The band played. The audience, who hadn't sat back down, cheered. And Denny turned his back to the audience and shook his massive rump at them.

Early on Denny, filled with inspiration, danced even harder than he did the first song. But he was wearing out. Sweat was melting the make-up off his face. "Oh my God," said Skinny. "That fat son-of-a-bitch is going to have a heart attack and ruin my set." Looking at Denny struggle with the song, I feared Skinny might be right. Alan must have noticed Denny's slowing, too. He stepped away from his desk and danced beside Denny. The audience went crazy. When the song ended, Alan lifted Denny's arm like a boxer who just won a fight. "Dancing Denny, ladies and gentlemen." He then cut to commercial.

Skinny looked at his watch. "We have eight minutes left. If Alan brings me right up, we cool." He bounced up and down while going over his set list. Returning from the break, Denny sat beside Alan at the desk.

"We're back," Alan said when cued. "Denny, that was really something. How long have you been dancing?"

Skinny about had a conniption fit. "He's paneling! What possible information could he hope to obtain from this guy?"

It wasn't the information Alan was looking for. It was laughs. Alan asked Denny questions that one would ask a serious ballerina, and the audience got the joke. Although, listening to Denny's serious answers, I'm not sure whether he did.

Alan asked him where he studied dance. What kind of diet and exercise regiment he had to commit to. Denny spoke of how dancing was the physical manifestation of one's soul, free to express itself. The audience applauded. Alan, having mined the interview for all it was worth, introduced Skinny with four minutes left on the show.

Skinny stormed the stage, shouting, "Look at all the white people." Denny made a face. "How come only black people proud of speaking bad English. I ain't talking like no white man. You don't hear Asians doing that. 'Me uh na talky rike uh da rite man.'" A few polite chuckles, but the bit tanked. Skinny was talking much too fast. He tried to squeeze eight minutes into four, and it just didn't work. He took a deep breath. "My old lady want me to go to Paris, France. I said what they got there?"

A waitress dropped a tray. You could hear glasses break. The whole audience turned to look at the accident. Skinny froze in disbelief.

Alan yelled from his desk, "Just put those anywhere." The audience laughed. He followed with, "We better break for commercial so the club can afford new glassware."

Skinny's set was over, two minutes after it started.

After the show, Skinny, Denny and I sat in the lounge, each having a drink. It was awkward because Denny wanted to relive the show and Skinny, of course, did not. "This fucking business," Skinny kept muttering.

Sensing the bitterness, Denny felt obliged to offer some wisdom. "Buddhism teaches us that if we practice only to become enlightened, we never will. You lose what the practice means trying to reach a goal. But when you believe in the way, practice for practice sake, then you attain enlightenment."

Skinny's retort was succinct. "Shut up, fool."

Denny smiled. "Let me put it another way. Show business is like fishing. If you worry about catching more fish, or bigger fish than someone else, it's no fun. But if you just enjoy the day; enjoy the fact that you're doing something you love, you can be happy."

Skinny refused to look at Denny. He took a drink of beer and mumbled, "Your fat ass would sink a fishing boat." Denny's advice was valid, of course, but I saw Skinny's side, too. You feel more pressure fishing when you're hungry.

As the audience paid their bills, the lounge quickly filled with people, most of them wanting to talk with Denny. I kept peering toward the showroom door, waiting for Lauren to enter. I felt nervous. Skinny sat quietly, as the masses bypassed him to pay tribute to Denny. A man with a crew cut turned to Skinny and offered a, "You weren't bad either."

"High praise," Skinny said, excusing himself to the greenroom.

Kevin and his crew finally entered the lounge, with Lauren speaking to one of the wives. I rose and met them at the bar but soon returned when Kevin suggested I introduce his customers to Denny. After a few minutes of Denny regaling them with the strategy and thought process behind his dancing, Kevin said, "We better get going. Some of us have to work in the morning." That comment, of course, was directed at me.

"Oh," I said, glancing at Lauren. No effort was made to hide my disappointment.

"I drove separately," she said. "If you still want to have that drink."

"Absolutely!" I reached for my wallet. "I'll get you another vodka tonic."

"Diet Coke," she corrected. "I do have a long drive home at some point."

I wanted to get back with Lauren. This I knew. And to my surprise, it didn't depress me. To end up where I started, after all I'd been through, should've made the whole thing seem pointless. But it didn't. Things were different now. I wasn't playing it safe, or going along with the crowd. If there is destiny, how would God communicate it to me? By making me want to do certain things. This is what I wanted.

Kevin shook my hand good-bye. "You're welcome," he said, discreetly. "Try not to screw it up this time."

"I won't," I said. And I certainly didn't intend to.

HAPPY ENDING
February 2

The baby slept in its little cage, or crib as they liked to call it, with five sets of eyes staring at it.

"Ahh. She's so cute," Lauren whispered. "How old is she again?"

"Six months, twelve days," Stacy replied softly.

"Oh, I can't wait until we have ours," Cindy said. She and Pea recently announced that "they" were two months pregnant.

"You're going to love it, Pea," Wally said.

Pea put his arm around Cindy. They had returned from Holland right before Christmas. Pea would receive his master's in the spring. Initially, he planned to continue on with his PhD, but now with his family growing he was fielding offers from animal health companies.

Off to the side I read Wally's newspaper. Denny's essay on Martin Luther King Day had run right before the holiday, and it dominated the letters to the editor page even now, a week later. The opinions ranged from him being a prophet to him being a Judas, and almost all calling for him to reveal himself. "Have you guys been reading these letters to the editor?"

"Oh my God," Wally said. "People want to lynch whoever wrote that article."

"Shhh," Stacy said. "You'll wake the baby."

Matilda wiggled for a moment, the five voyeurs held their breath. Matilda opened her eyes and screamed at the top of her lungs. Wally immediately sprung into panic mode. "Sweetie," he said to Stacy, "do you want me to take her?"

"No, we're fine," she said, picking up Matilda. "The girls and I can handle it." I would have rather taken a fishhook to my eyebrow than have to hear that screaming, yet no one else seemed to mind. It actually seemed pleasing to Lauren and Cindy.

Wally put his face near Matilda's. "Did we get scared? Is all the people scaring us? It's okay, Mommy and Daddy loves us. Mommy and

Daddy loves us."

This caused Lauren and Cindy to chime in. "We not going to hurt you. We just wanted to see how pretty you is…"

Pea sat down beside me. "Jesus Christ," he whispered.

"You better not start acting like that after you have yours," I said, also in a low voice, but for no reason. Between the screaming and the baby talk, I could have spoken into a megaphone and not have been heard.

The baby would not stop wailing. Stacy sniffed her little butt. "I think she needs her diaper changed."

"Did she make a boom boom?" Wally said into the little girl's face. "Did she? Does she need her dipey changed? Yes she does. Yes she does."

I looked at Pea. "Don't worry," he said. "I won't."

Finally, action was taken. The ladies took Matilda into the nursery to change and feed her. Wally watched them walk down the hall, fighting the urge to join them. "I'm telling you, Pea," he said, staring longingly into the empty crib. "You're going to love it."

Wally went on and on about the joys of fatherhood, and the things to watch out for, as Pea politely nodded and said "Uh huh." After several minutes of this, I broke in. "So Wally, you read that article on Martin Luther King Day. What'd you think?"

"It made some good points, but you can see why it was submitted anonymously. People are pissed."

"Who do you think wrote it?" I asked.

"Stacy and I were discussing it. We think it's a high profile black leader. Somebody who wants to get their message across without hurting their own position in the black community. Or maybe even a black conservative."

Knowing the truth, I couldn't help but be amused. "Maybe it's just some big fat white guy who fears that if he signed his name it would lose all credibility."

Wally laughed. "That would be hilarious. But I think whoever wrote it, is clearly an insider in black politics."

Pea, who hadn't read the essay, changed the subject. "Hey Vic, I heard you moved in with Lauren."

"Yep. I moved in about three weeks ago."

"Things must be getting pretty serious then," Wally said.

"Why do say that?"

"She wouldn't let you live with her unless she thought you would get married, right?" Wally asked.

Is that what she thought? I had been spending all my evenings over there because it was fun. When I mentioned that my parents were kicking me out, she said that I might as well just move in with her, since I was there all the time anyhow. Plus, with her new promotion she would have to travel a lot and felt better having me there to watch the house and feed her cats. It seemed like common sense. Had I been tricked? "I don't think we're really thinking marriage at this point."

"You might not be," Pea said. "But why else would she let you mooch off her."

"It's not like it's costing her anything, Pea. She doesn't give me an allowance," I said. "I have a job now. I write jokes for that television show."

"How much does that pay?" Wally asked.

"It pays seventy-five dollars a week. Plus, I get free food and drinks when I'm at the club."

"Seventy-five dollars a week, and you expect me to believe she's not supporting you," Pea said.

"I also shine shoes two days a week," I added, without mentioning that all proceeds go to the homeless or others in need. It didn't need mentioning because the most I ever made in a week was $30. "Besides, trust me, I'm earning that room and board. She makes me go to her crazy church."

"That's no big deal," Pea said. "I have to do that."

"Yeah, but she goes to one of those quote unquote fun churches. With a rock band, and a minister walking around with a wireless mike, working the room. 'How you doing?' 'What's shaking Bob?' 'Looking good Susie.' It's all just a little too cute for me. 'Look at us. We're having fun because we love God,'" I said in a very patronizing voice. "I hate all that stuff. I'm Catholic."

"I thought you were becoming a Buddhist."

"That's not the point. The point is that I'm not getting a free ride here. I'm making sacrifices too. They actually have a group who perform sketches every week. Adults, mind you."

"Get used to it," Pea said. "That's probably the church you'll be married in."

Before I could protest, Lauren walked down the hall carrying Matilda in her arms. "Are you talking about our church?"

"Yeah," I said, nervous about what she might have overheard.

"You guys should join us some week," Lauren said. "It's so much fun. Vic and I love it. They have a band, and perform little plays."

"Vic was telling us about that," Pea said. "He writes jokes for that other show, he should help write those sketches."

"That's a good idea," Lauren said. "Would you like that, Vic?"

"He said he would." Pea struggled to keep a straight face.

"Great," Lauren said. "I bet they'll let you perform in them, too. Now you guys definitely have to come."

"We wouldn't miss it for the world," Wally said.

Matilda cooed in Lauren's arms. "She is the most adorable thing in the world," Lauren told Wally.

Wally beamed. "We kind of like her."

Stacy carried a trivial pursuit game when she re-entered the living room with Cindy. "We were just talking Lauren, about how much we like you. You round out our little group perfectly."

Lauren glowed in the kindness. Cindy punched my thigh. "Somebody had to settle this guy down. Didn't they, Vic?"

Heat rushed to my ears. I forced a chuckle. This was more than just friendly tidings, an agenda was afoot.

"Lauren, let's see how Vic looks holding that baby," Cindy said.

"No, that's all right," I said. "Lauren's enjoying herself."

"Have you ever held Matilda?" Stacy asked, opening the trivial pursuit box.

"Yeah, the last time I was here." It took about ten seconds for Matilda to start bawling and Wally to take her back. Not a great first impression for either of us.

"You gotta do it more than once to get used to it."

There is really no polite way to refuse holding a friend's baby. Lauren handed Matilda to me. I held her secure to my body and gently rocked her. The room closed in as my friends stood over me. Matilda's little fingers wiggled.

"She likes you," Wally said.

"Be careful, Lauren," Cindy said. "He'll be wanting one of his own soon."

Lauren didn't speak, but her answer was in her smile. It was in the way she gently fixed my hair before kissing my ear. She loved me. This is it, the happy ending. They lived happily ever after. *Oh God, what have I done?*

THE END

See how it all got started. *Through the Turn* is the second book in the Vic Walker series. The first, *The Big Cookie,* takes place when Vic, Wally and Pea are in college.

The Big Cookie

Being single is scary for many of us. But the mild anxiety most people associate with dating balloons into full-blown terror for Wally. A shy and insecure college student, he is convinced that he will die alone if he doesn't find a wife by gradu- ation. But he is too timid to even ask for a date. He assumes that no girl would want him because he has committed the unpardonable sin of being unattractive in a shallow world. He is convinced that finding love is more difficult when you're ugly—especially if you're looking for someone who isn't.

To make matters worse, his best friend Vic is constantly involving him in complicated schemes to impress beautiful women. Together, they bumble and humiliate themselves through intercollegiate absurdity after absurdity, all in their distinct personal quests to wrap their minds around the opposite sex and the whole notion of physical attraction.

From the hallowed halls of Purdue University to the sunny beaches of Acapulco, *The Big Cookie* captures the "laugh out loud" humor of trying to be something you're not and the requisite anxiety it causes. It also reminds us, that being single would be a lot more fun, if you just knew it wouldn't last forever.

Available at www.ScottDunnComedy.com or Amazon.com

Scott Dunn

For author biography and other information,
please visit **www.ScottDunnComedy.com**